FOG

A NOVEL BY
EDAN BENN EPSTEIN

An idyllic tale of mayhem set in the California Redwoods

December

The road worker from the county was the first to notice that something was terribly wrong. Fog had lifted sufficiently to see the road, but not what lay beyond. Or below. A seasoned road worker or cop could see the black marks, the displaced rocks, could smell the leaking fuel and carburetor smoke. There were no guard rails on this stretch of Highway 1. The road snaked its way against the ocean, ten miles north of Klamath, at least a mile from the nearest habitation.

The county worker suspected that a car had sailed over the cliff during the night and had crashed below. Every year or so, this was bound to happen. Everyone's afraid of the Tsunami, ignorant or dismissive of the real risk out here.

Eventually, everyone would be able to see it, the disaster below. But even then it would be a sonovabitch to remove it, even the body, for the car would be impaled against the rocks, abutting a jagged cliff, buffeted by the constant waves. Until the moment it sinks altogether. If it's still there, it's overtime pay for sure, he thought, with little enthusiasm. He picks up his radio to make the call.

The following May

Rain persisted for the third straight night. It fell from the unseen places, from the mists and from the flat gray sky. It turned the rare barren slopes into mud slips that choked the narrow hillside lanes overlooking the invisible ocean. It fell by turns in mists and torrents, flooding the trails, sluicing down gutter ways.

The rain slowed Ari's progress towards his home, two miles north of Trinidad harbor, through a winding verdant road and onto a flat dirt lane. Even at close range, his home and his manicured lawn was hidden by the hanging wet canopy of branch and leaf. Ari felt witness to yet immune from the elements. They were his to enjoy from his comfortable arm chair, watching the rainwater slide down his window, drench his lawn, and fill his ears. The sounds grew louder.

During an average commute it takes an hour for Ari to reach the college south of Eureka. This is without traffic; but there almost never is any traffic, except where the 101 passes directly through the streets of Eureka, a town that persists in disappointing him in its ugly junkiness. Even the Victorian style buildings downtown have a mean, crowded, and forlorn appearance.

Ari escapes Eureka and heads out on 101 south, past the open green fields to a barely noticeable turn out for the college where he teaches, hidden in its own gentle tree laden world. He doubts he will ever teach at the larger, more prestigious university in Arcata. But this was what he always wanted; a modest yet respectable teaching job conveniently located at the idyllic ends of the earth. That's what Humboldt County was, at least for him; the convenient end of the earth, Brigadoon covered in mists. The hotter the inland frying was during summer, the foggier and colder it persisted in Trinidad and Patrick's Point, but also in Arcata, Orick, Klamath, and far to the north Eureka's smaller, evil twin, Crescent City, and so on along the craggy Redwood coast.

Humboldt County lives between the grasp of the Redwood giants on one side and the shivering gray salty sea on the other. Highway signs warned of possible tsunamis. Crescent City had suffered damage to its harbor and there were eight recorded deaths in 1964, significant for a town of barely a thousand people back then. In 2011, after the cataclysmic quake in Japan, Crescent City was hit again, though not as fiercely. Still, there was one recorded death; that of a foolhardy individual who was swept out to sea while attempting to video tape the event.

When returning home Ari glimpses the bottomless white blanket of endless fog, the ocean evident only from the smell of salt and sperm; Ari's thoughts turn to imagining the poor schmuck whose idle lark turned to panic and struggle and then despair as he likely realized that his very life was imperiled. Even worse was the probable realization that his entire existence culminated in a singular, futile instant of ultimate loss. People often seemed to lose their lives in the most ludicrously frightening ways.

Ari shook the images away. He considered that an irrational part of him expected to be protected by the surrounding mists and fog and rain, that he lived - comfortably now – beyond not just physical threats, but psychological and emotional ones as well. A finger of misty fog crept onto the road as if to greet him.

The next day, Thursday, was uncharacteristically warm and sunny, though rain was predicted again for that night. Ari stoically proctored his finals. Both his classes were sections of Introduction to Cost Accounting. He had already taught this class so many times with so little variation that he knew and anticipated without even thinking about it, every single point, every example, and certainly every joke (few and weak as they were) for every single lecture of this course as well as for all the courses he taught. There were even times when it felt like he had been teaching in a black out and he had little recollection of a morning or an evening. Once or twice, he had even experienced himself "coming

7

to" in the middle of a class. He would lose his place and stood looking at the white board, hands in pockets, trying not to let on. Thoughtfully, he would stroke his chin and look at the book, look out archly at his students, smile, and pick up perfectly from wherever he had left off.

He was engaging and he knew it, when he was fully present. And he supposed he was almost exactly the same when he wasn't. When he was "on" he was helpful, useful, charming, and funny. He energized young minds to embrace business and to go forth and reshape the fluid, sustaining network of business and global wealth. Then there were other days when all of felt pointless and effete, merely abstract fundamentals that fell like toy ghosts upon bovine intellects, listless and unambitious cyber surfers, occupiers of cheap seats at a well-manicured, third rate institution. The best he hoped for on such days – like today – was a polite laugh and a couple of hot and vulnerable looking young women in the class.

Not that he was actually ever going to make a move on any of them. He agreed that moving forward he needed to keep his private appetites as separate from work as possible. Except, of course, for that one time. Or maybe two, if you counted the grown woman who came to see him after she graduated. Everyone knew about the "grown woman", for he had dutifully let the administration know. They appreciated his candor, if not his choices.

No one knew about the other one. No one would ever know. It was wrong and he knew it. And so he vowed never to repeat such behavior.

Ari had what he had characterized as a complicated relationship with his boss, Clarence "Bud" Cameron, the Dean of the Business Department. Cameron had actually told Ari quite often that he admired and valued his teaching skills and methods, as well as his reliability and timeliness when it came to his attendance, grading, and general adherence to college policies. Nonetheless, Ari felt that Cameron, an otherwise kindly, avuncular figure, was generally cool towards him. Though it had never been discussed openly, Ari was certain that it had to do with his disclosed affair with Catherine Lessor. But instead of

8

expressing his disappointment directly, Cameron instead chose to nudge Ari about "stepping up" - just a little bit, he said – outside of the classroom, for the welfare of the department and for the college. Ari was sure. More than once, Cameron reminded Ari, that "we pay you a full time salary, with benefits, for a part time job. You work three days a week, eight months a year. You're not getting rich, of course, but it's not a bad life, with a strong wage in a low price county. It's not unreasonable for us to ask that you help us once in a while on business that helps this school, and therefore, you as well". Something like that.

But Cameron never actually asked him to do anything, outside of showing up at a dinner once in a while. As for more responsibilities, Ari thought he might get to be the faculty advisor for the student accounting club. He was a popular instructor, after all. But no. Dirk Hoth had a lock on that. Did Cameron expect Ari to *ask* for work? He didn't think so. So therefore this was all about Catherine Lessor.

He walked into Cameron's outer office, a shared space with wood paneling. About five minutes late. This meeting was all that stood between him and going home where he could work on grading. He had a lot of work to do, but was planning on taking the night off, this being the last night of school and he had until Monday to finish the goddamn grades. Maybe he'd pick up a movie or two, listen to the rain. If he got bored, there was a woman in Smith River he might call. Maybe he'd see her tomorrow night, Friday night, after an honest day's work, grading.

"Hi Janie," he said, greeting the department secretary. He sat down, expecting Cameron to keep him waiting.

"Go on in, Professor Fisher. He's expecting you." Only Janie called him, Professor. He was only an Instructor. Cameron was leaning back in his swivel chair on the phone, but he quickly wrapped up. "Frank, I'll call you back later." Ari recognized the name of someone from the business office. "Ari, glad to see you. Have a seat." He came from around his desk and took a chair closer to Ari. Even with all the supposed budget cuts, how come Bud Cameron had a larger office with what looked like his own secretary? Was this Harvard? "Glad the semester's over?"

"Oh, you know, it'll be nice to be completely loose for a bit. It's not like it's so grueling, Bud."

"Yes, yes, that's right," Cameron agreed. "That's right," he repeated. "Yes…we have it pretty good, I'd say." Ari sensed Cameron might as well have said, *you* have it pretty good.

"Yes, I do. But I was thinking of taking on that fund accounting class, if you still want me to."

"Maybe…Good to know. But I need your help with something else, more immediate, actually."

"Really? Tell me. The semester is over, like you said," Ari pointed out, instantly wishing he had kept that needless observation to himself.

"That's right," Cameron agreed, impatiently. "But the school has expenses and needs all the time."

"True!" Ari piped up.

"Of course, we're funded by the state, but you know very well that the state budget is in the shit hole right now. Education is being cut right and left, even though it hasn't affected us in the business department quite as much. Now we've always been grateful for alumni and other private donations, but now more so than ever. Otherwise," he said, leveling Ari with a look, "We may need to start cutting classes, or even non-tenured faculty, Ari."

"Right." That was a direct, goddamn threat, Ari thought.

"Don't worry, Ari," Cameron said, leaning back, his chair creaking. "I'm not asking you to donate money," he said, smiling. Ari did not smile back. "I do need your help though in collecting it."

"Sure. Just tell me what you need me to do."

"Really, Ari, it's the simplest thing in the world. We've already done the 'telethon' if you will. All I am going to ask you to do is what you do best and enjoy the most, Ari."

"Teach a class?"

"Take a donor out to dinner. A woman donor, Ari. It will be a very charming evening. We have all but secured a very sizable check, make that *very* sizable check. It will be enough to guarantee retention of our part time non-tenured faculty, like you, Ari."

"I see."

"She's a widow. Her grandson graduated from her two years ago. He was to matriculate into HSU, but then he died suddenly. Tragically."

"In the tsunami?" Ari offered, pointing upwards, to Crescent City.

"Is that funny, Ari?"

"No. Probably not, Bud. What happened?" Ari asked, trying to sound sincere and sober now.

"He drove his car off Highway One, over the cliffs. Last December. You might have heard about that. It made the news."

"Oh, God. How horrible," He remembered the incident.

"Mrs. Ng is in town through Saturday --"

"Mrs Ing?"

"Yes, Victoria Ng. She's originally from Vietnam, I'd guess, as so many of our students are, nowadays."

"Yes."

"Of course. Those of us who involved in the Founders' activities have heard of her." Those of us who play team and who give a shit about our school have all heard of her, is what he might have said, is what Ari decided. And he would have had so much more respect for Bud if in fact he really had spoken his mind like that. He let it pass. "The delicate part's already done," Cameron went on. "She came to us. We met with her. It's a done deal. But...you know as a goodwill gesture, as a class act, we took the hint that since she was at loose ends this Friday, we offered to find her someone to....accompany her."

"Tomorrow?"

"Yes. You catch on."

"What do you mean, 'accompany'?"

"Ari, it's nothing. Take her out to dinner. Take her to Turendotte, on our dime, of course. That's all. She's an intelligent woman. You should have no lack of conversation."

"How do you know I don't already have plans?"

"Do you?" Read a book. Watch a movie on his home big screen. Watch the rain. Cyber troll for bored and lonely women pining in Quincy, Fortuna, Smith River, even Weed. Driving was no problem.

"No, Bud. Just grading papers. Lots of them"

"Take a break from that."

"Well, in fact, I am planning on spending the day with my son on Saturday, Bud. He's leaving the country for two years on a Peace Corps mission."

"Ah yes, that's right. They still have that going on, the Peace Corps. Good for him. Outstanding."

"So that's why I need to finish my grading tomorrow."

"Makes sense. It's Simon. Right?"

"Simon. That's correct." At that moment, Ari did not like the idea of Bud Cameron even knowing his son's name.

"That's wonderful, Ari. Of course it is a very long time to be without your boy."

"Yes."

"He's probably just a bit younger than my son."

"Must be nice to have a son who's a cop."

"You think? I worry about him, you know. Even though he's not going far away, like Simon." Ari merely nodded and grunted, restraining himself from pointing out that there was likely little danger to a CHP officer here in Humboldt County. Cameron continued. "Anyway, I'm really sorry about the last minute notice, Ari, I grant you that. But our donor, she actually requested you specifically, young man. Mrs. Ng. I would have picked you regardless, but now I really need your help."

"She picked me?"

"You were her grandson's favorite instructor. Leon Ng."

"Oh."

"I'm not surprised about that. But I really need you to play team on this."

"I had a feeling you'd say that."

"Did you? Is there a reason you can't go to your office right now, or even go home and just bang these out, the paper's you're grading, today and tomorrow morning? And Sunday? Grades aren't due until Tuesday morning, you know that."

It'll be damned hard if I decide to hike up around Orick for a day or two, Ari thought. "No. Probably not. It's just a surprise, is all. I suppose you feel I owe it to the team." Cameron just looked at him. "Well…..Bud, I agree."

"Good. Glad to hear you say that."

"So…fine…so what am I supposed to do exactly?"

"Be charming. Not necessarily too charming, if you know what I mean," and Cameron winked at him with good humor. You mean, don't fuck her, Bud, is what he thought. "Mrs. Ng will be expecting you to pick her up where she's staying at the Comfort Suites near the airport. It's all arranged."

"I know where it is."

"Just take her to dinner and charge it to us. Whatever you want. Take her to Turendotte, or whatever your favorite restaurant is. Listen to her wax on about her dead son."

"You're quite the sentimentalist, Bud."

"Just be charming and interested, a good listener, and all that."

"Alright. I guess I'm flattered. Anything else?"

Cameron just looks at him for a moment. "This is very important to us, Ari. This is not a difficult task, I think, but we're really counting on you. We know you won't let us down."

Ari was back on the road by three. He loved the serene near empty outer parking lot near the campus entrance, and he loved the conceit that he had found a place on the edge of the world; a comfortable one of course, with indoor plumbing, lighting, and heating. He looked up at the tall placid trees that flanked every part of the campus. There were twenty seven hours left before he had to dispatch his duty of babysitting some self-important elder donor who no doubt would spend the entire evening eulogizing her beloved grandson.

Ari had just turned 52, was divorced, unencumbered, self-sufficient, and self-determined. He became a CPA, the fastest, cheapest, safest way to obtain a prestigious and lucrative career; no law school, no medical school, no graduate studies at all. He passed the exam in two tries straight out of school. Ari was considered handsome and rugged, premature gray and bright green eyes. He put in his two years at a then Big Eight CPA firm, enough to get his requisite experience to obtain his license. Ari was asked to stay on for a third year, but left instead to work for a regional firm before finally leaving public accounting to go work internally for a large engineering firm. He climbed as high as manager, right below the CFO and settled there with a good salary, great benefits, and as much responsibility as he wanted. Then he married a sensible, sharply attractive woman who worked in quality assurance, one with a respectable income of her own.

Sabrina seemed well enough adjusted apart from a tendency to talk a great deal about her college days as a dancer and how she might have pursued it further but she did not want a life of living on the edge and so she became an engineer instead. She hated it but it did impress her family and made her independent, and as a member of quality. Whenever she spoke of it at a dinner party over her third glass of Chardonnay, animated and loud, there was supportive laughter all around, for she was being ironic and self-depreciating. Ari was quite aware that whereas Sabrina pointed out every single time he told a story more than once, she herself had no clue how many times she did the same thing, glass in hand, but that was something that he was never going to tell her.

His job was easy and he and Sabrina purchased a large and comfortable home in the early nineties, outside of San Jose, which appreciated greatly during the Clinton and early Bush years. Prosperity and innovation had swept most of the nation. Crime went down. At the time of their home purchase, the Russians had become allies, even if precariously so, while freedom seemed to sweep new part of the world from eastern Europe to central Asia. All was well except in a few

14

obscure parts of the world, like Rwanda, Kosovo, Chechnya, Somalia, Congo, North Korea, Iraq, Afghanistan, China, Burma, Syria, Yemen, Lybia, India, Columbia, Mexico, and the invisible desperate millions even in the United States. And the list, Ari realized, could be extended indefinitely. Yes, it would be enough for him to be able to name just a few of these countries by name to show that he cared and to impress others at campus mixers of his worldliness. Sabrina and Ari had earned tax savings by giving regularly to charities both within and outside the United States. Ari, on his own, decided to continue the practice.

Their son Simon was about to join the Peace Corps. He would soon be on his way to help build school houses and teach poor Guatemalan children. Ari was genuinely proud of his son, but also found him a bit idealistic or maybe just on the make for adventure.

Ari cultivated hobbies like hiking, canoeing, and camping, though Sabrina did not share in these. (They did, however, ski and play tennis together.) With his college friend, Albert, the lone remaining vestige of his young adult buddies, he went backpacking and fly fishing in Oregon at least once a year. These were manly occupations that compensated for the lucrative, but admittedly sterile work he had chosen.

He fondly remembered his early sex life with his good looking, responsive wife, which was easy and efficient. Such memories now often aroused anger which in certain strange moments heightened his solitary arousal. Someone else was fucking her now.

When Sabrina had brought up the subject of children, Ari had been hesitant and wanted to wait, if only a couple of years, hoping secretly to stretch the time frame indefinitely. At first, his wife had gone along with his wishes but it was clear that she was not happy.

All of that changed when he and Albert went hiking one weekend in the Sierras. They were higher up the mountain than they had ever been, and they were now well above the snow level, for there had been a late snow in June that year. The hike had gone well until the tiniest moment of absent mindedness when Ari stepped upon a slick piece of ice that he had taken for snow. The slip and fall seemed to

15

happen in slow motion, yet Ari was unable to correct himself or even to comprehend that his body was out of control. He slid feet first, face down in the snowy slope. His descent was finally stopped by a boulder and cushioned by a snow bank. Ari raised his head, confused by the shouting above. A long time seemed to have passed. He managed to look up and estimate that he was maybe fifty feet from the trail. So he raised his arm, his fist, to signify that he was alright. Albert was still speaking. What? "Don't move, Ari. Don't move! Not yet," he was saying. Albert assiduously instructed him to climb straight up, if he could, digging into the snow, looking ahead to avoid any ice. Slowly.

At first, it didn't seem as if he was making any progress. The last few feet to the trail were the most harrowing. Straight up it seemed. Ari could barely feel his hands anymore. Albert coached him towards a a place where Ari could get his grip. But then he began to slip again his breath caught in his throat, hot crystals of snow and ice mashing into his face. And then just for an instant, Ari held the intrusive suggestion in his head to simply let go and tumble into the abyss, to sleep. He wondered if he would even feel a thing. Albert's voice snapped his attention back to his task. Fear gripped him once more as he still could not feel his hands. "Don't you take me down with you, you bastard!" Albert barked, but he didn't sense any real fear in his friend's voice. Ari managed to sling a leg over the trail and he rested, trying to catch his breath.

Almost miraculously, it seemed, Ari had neither twisted nor mangled any limbs. Apart from his hands tingling and burning and his jeans being thoroughly soaked, he was okay. Soon, the two of them reached a fork in the trail which they followed downwards, quickly descending below the snow line. They made it back to the car three hours later as evening was falling. Ari was exhausted and sore.

"Remember when I shouted at you up there, not to move? After you fell, I mean," Albert asked him.

"Yeah. I think that rings a tiny little bell. What happened?"

"Well I'm glad you didn't ask me about it at the time. But had you slid two or three more feet to your right, you would probably have sailed right off the cliff."

16

Ari looked at him and looked back out at the defrosting front window. "That's what I figured," he said. In his mind, he profusely thanked his friend, yet he remained quiet. Ari thought he might well owe Albert his life. And yet he vaguely resented Albert, because he had slipped and Albert had not and he felt foolish. "Well what was the point of telling me now?" he muttered. But he gave his friend a sheepish grin so as not to offend him. His slip had embarrassed him, but so did his resentment. He certainly did not share with Albert his surreal moment of longing to fall into the abyss.

He mentioned nothing whatsoever about his slip on the mountain with his wife. Following the incident, however, Ari thought about how much ordinary danger he routinely survived; momentary cell phone distractions on the highway, narrowly avoiding high speed collisions; stepping out from his car onto a busy thoroughfare and feeling the carbon wind of a passenger bus narrowly missing him; or even inadvertently pointing the plastic cork of a champagne bottle at himself, the cork bouncing sharply off his head, inches from exploding forever through his eye. Seconds and inches between life and death, between being physically whole and traumatically maimed; these were the conveniently forgotten pivots haunting him in the days following the hiking incident.

Instead of disclosing his narrow escape to Sabrina, he decided he was ready to start a family. She never questioned to his face his sudden change of her. She merely accepted it, gratefully.

The next time Ari had a brush with his own mortality was to all appearances absolutely no threat whatsoever. It came and went as a shadow, a momentary madness, or just merely a perverse train of thought, quickly to dissolve in distraction. It was the moment when he first arrived, newly divorced, free and duly appointed at the college, the fresh and unencumbered new owner of his newly furnished dream home, secluded and silent, with its view of the ocean and its own private woods. On that day, in that hour, that moment – as Ari Fisher approached his own front door - the very moment of which he had long dreamed and towards which he had strived - at that simple, perfect moment, Ari felt a heaviness billow through him like a harness of fog.

He inserted the key, turned, and stepped across his chilly threshold. He switched on the light and threw his keys on the tray near the door. They fell instead loudly to the floor. Ari turned the light back off. It was late afternoon and the murky day was already waning leaving a bluish smoky hue in the room. He opened the sliding door to let the air in, took his shoes off, sat back in his recliner, and it was then, this perfect moment, it was at that moment that he decided that although he did not relish the idea of killing himself, that perhaps he was in fact, already dead.

The phone rings but stops as soon as he gets home from his meeting with Cameron. Ari takes out his cell, realizes it's off and turns it back on. A moment later, his cell predictably rings, and he was relieved to see it was his son.

"Simon!"

"Hey, dad."

"What's going on? I'm glad you called. It's been a little while, huh."

"Just checking up on you, pop," Ari waited for Simon to continue. "I've been busy, but I've been thinking about you. I haven't heard from you either, dad."

"Checking up on your old man, eh. So what are you doing? Are you all excited? Can you hardly stand it?"

"Yeah, dad. I'm all set now. School's done. One last orientation this weekend. And then I'm outta here next Tuesday."

"Amazing," Ari said in a flat tone. "So…Will I see you before you leave?"

"Can you come down over the weekend? I like coming to see you , but I've got way too much to do to get ready."

"I understand, son," Ari said, feeling disappointed and spoiled. "Yes, I'll make it down to see you as soon as I am done with grading."

"OK."

"I know you have other people you need to say goodbye to," Ari said, thinking of Sabrina mostly. He did not particularly want to see her just now though of course it was appropriate and he had to step for his son. There was also his girlfriend. Tabitha? "What's your girlfriend's name?"

"Dana? We're split up. I'm on my own. On my own and on my way."

"Now that's like your old man," Ari said with feeling that surprised himself.

"Yeah, kind of....I'm really happy about what I'm doing."

"Mm hmm."

"So when do you think you'll make it down here?"

"When exactly are you leaving?"

"Tuesday, dad. I told you, the seventeenth."

"No, but I mean when exactly...What time?"

"The flight leaves at midnight. So Wednesday morning, technically. But please tell me you're not going to wait until Tuesday night to come see me at the airport."

"I'm not saying that at all" Ari retorted, feeling testy. "I just don't know yet. I have to look at my schedule. Plus, I have a lot of grading to do."

"You teach accounting."

"And general business and management. I assigned a paper, you know."

"But you also have to come down for my going away, send off, dad. It's Saturday night. "

"Where?" Ari said. How could he almost forget to tell me a thing like that?

"It starts at La Monica's. At seven. Remember? I'll email the address to you. And text it."

"Please."

"And then after that at...."

"Your mother's?"

"Uh huh. She's gonna be there at the dinner, too, you know."

"I figured that, Simon. Of course. That's fine."

"Cool."

"Simon, which airline are you taking?"

"You want to take me to the airport?" Simon asked archly.

19

"I want to make sure you're flying safely."

"Air Mexico, dad. I told you."

"Really? Now see, could you get down there on United or something like that?"

"Dad, it's a group flight and it's already arranged. I'm leaving Tuesday! Besides, United sucks!"

"No they don't. But that's not the point."

"Right. The point is that it's a done deal, dad. I'm going to Guatemala. The flight there should be the safest part!" Simon added brightly.

"Is that supposed to make me feel better about your safety?"

"Come on, dad. Everything checks out. There's risks in everything, dad. There's risks in being alive. There's risks to driving down the freeway."

"Yes, Simon, but this is a little different, I'd say," Ari retorted, secretly agreeing with his son. Even if you stayed in bed all day long, there was a high risk of getting bed sores, muscle deconditioning, back injury, falling out of bed. Home invasion!

"Dad, I'm leaving next Tuesday," Simon repeated, as if that settled the issue.

"Alright, son. Send me the information," he sighed. "I'll call you tomorrow."

"Good. Love you, dad."

"See you soon, son."

Ari sat at his desk and set out to read some twenty odd sophomore papers on business and management principles at companies they would likely never be considered to work for. Catherine Lessor was one of the few exceptions. He had worked steadily for over an hour when he distracted himself by looking her up on the internet. She was hard to find because her name was common. But he knew how to find her, at her public relations firm in Walnut Creek, perfect teeth and blonde hair, always well dressed and professional looking. Leon Ng was actually much easier to find because of the tragic and lurid circumstances

20

of his untimely death. He was actually a big round faced kid with glasses and an unsmiling high school year book photo that had been used when the story of his death was published. It was as if he had been photographed by someone who had just told him that one day soon he would drive over a cliff. Ari squinted at the photo but could not bring himself to recognize the kid.

His students were of two general ages. Most were traditional 18 and 19 year olds, long limbed frightened children merely, with a thin veil of irksome bravado or indifference, some of them. But all of them were there presumably by choice, or whatever choice was left when one considered they did not qualify or could not afford to go to Humboldt state, or had no clue what they would do to earn a living. Most of them would never go to the university; perhaps half would never even finish their first two years at the college. Aside from these callow youths, as Ari viewed them, there were also the "grown-ups", usually thirty some things, working full time, or perhaps newly unemployed or underemployed, dislocated by the recession.

Catherine was clearly amongst these latter folks. Her intention was to matriculate into the university with a broadcast journalism major and a minor in business. Typically, Ari would catch himself judging business and accounting majors as lacking in imagination - like himself. Yet those like Catherine, on the other hand, who dared to pursue something bold and exciting - like broadcast journalism – these folks instead he dismissed as impractical and feckless. Except for Catherine.

She was also married, an unsavory detail that Cameron didn't know about. At least he hoped Bud didn't know about that. But she had no children. She had worked a few small jobs for years and before that she had aspired to go to nursing or veterinary school. Instead, she had married one of the few truly wealthy men in Humboldt County, who owned a great deal of the remaining commercial timberland in the area.

Now she was bored, restless, and aimless. Both she and her husband had in fact already had several routine affairs. She was clearly bound for the university and a variety of doors might still be open to her, especially amongst the smaller businesses that weren't obsessed with hiring cheap, malleable new grads. But broadcasting? Really? And yet he sensed it would be unwise to count her out for anything.

Upon his first look at Catherine in his class and he wondered whether she was some spoiled woman who felt she deserved a degree without the messy inconvenience of having to work for it, provided of course that she at least dressed well. He realized he did not like her. Even after she diligently and persistently took notes, Ari still wondered why she was there. But that much did not greatly trouble him as he was inclined to wonder the same about many of his students.

His dream job as a college instructor would have been so much more to his liking, he mused, if only he had no students and taught no classes. This was not really true, but all he preferred to do now was to stroll the edges of campus or to sit by the brook on any day that school was not in session. Ari was spoiled and he knew it. He was spoiled, he agreed, not Catherine Lessor.

They had their first extended conversation after she had aced her first exam in his financial accounting class. Rather, the narrative was more about how she decided to go back to school, which progressed into how Ari got into teaching. She told him how helpful he was, much more so than most, and how she was likely to seek out more of Ari's help and encouragement, because she did not mind admitting that she needed it. Throughout the conversation, Catherine mentioned her husband several times, never by name, but nonetheless it deflated Ari's fantasies.

Over the course of the next year, Catherine took two more classes with Ari. Despite minimal eye contact, all focus on her notes, he noticed, she began to frequent his office hours on what appeared as the thinnest of pretexts; a minor clarification on an assignment, or a speculative question on untested subject matter. When Ari realized that she might show up at any time he made a habit of always arriving at this scheduled hours on time and staying late until he had to leave for class. He congratulated himself on being conscientious enough to take his office hours seriously. Eventually, she started dropping by just to say Hello, with no pretext whatsoever.

Because she had already taken a few courses and was able to successfully test for her other GE requirements, it took her only a year for her to complete her associate degree. She left. Several months passed without hearing from her and Ari felt the loss of possibility. But just before she started at HSU, he received a call from her inviting him to join her for a drink. After their disastrous evening together, he found himself thinking of her, restlessly, with no real desire to ever see her again, but with a childish need instead to erase the memory of what had happened.

Instead of refocusing on his grading, Ari downloaded an action spy movie on his 42" flat screen. He sat through the first half hour, hand clenched and poised upon his remote until with a gnash of teeth her turned it off. He knew he was supposed to be relaxing, feeling care free, celebrating the end of another semester, but it wasn't over of course, not until he finished grading, not until he finished baby-sitting for Bud Cameron. A light rain began to fall. He turned the movie off. The wind picked up. He opened the drapes all the way to look out onto his little yard. And he turned out the light.

That one time he was with her he found to his horror that he could not do it. When the coiled flesh failed to come to life, Ari began to despair, feeling ashamed and powerless. Catherine thinly disguised her disappointment (and contempt, no doubt) with brisk efficiency. Don't worry about it, she said. It happens. Promptly, she offered to accept Ari into her mouth to which he gratefully agreed. The consolation prize. And it worked. All he had to do was to watch this high spirited creature level (debase) herself to the level of his dick. It was the sheen of her lip gloss that put her over the top. Catherine Lessor, the gorgeous, self-assured, and very married woman, resembled a whore.

Afterwards, she expressed the desire for a drink. This was in a small motel in Patrick's Point. (The kind where she wasn't likely to meet her husband she said, bemused). Then she disappeared into the shower. Listening to the sterile, efficient sound of the hot water, Ari wanted nothing more than to suddenly blink his eyes and to listen to the rain upon his roof and to witness it fall in his yard. His rain. But first, he would take a shower.

23

Ari listened to the rain happening right now. Unlike the explosion of techno sound and color from his television or computer, the rain was vital, a living thing, forged in the sky, received by the earth.

What had he expected from Catherine? And from himself? Her generosity, if that's what it was, made him feel like a hooker's John. If he could have foreseen a week earlier that Catherine Lessor would give him a full on blow job, he would have felt exalted with anticipation. He would not have foreseen that he would feel empty, vaguely mocked.

Unable either to work or relax it occurred to Ari to call Simon back and tell his son that he was proud of him. That he loved him. That he admired his son for doing a noble thing and for taking a worthy risk in his life, for seeking adventure with purpose. For being of service. Good reasons. Or? Was the boy merely running away? Delaying responsibilities? Hiding? Tell your son you are proud of him. Whether you know you mean it or not. Tell him. I love you, son, is what he thought to himself, sitting in the silence before the rain crept back into his mind.

The home phone interrupted Ari to let him know he had a text message. Always the thought intruded upon him, maybe it's her, come to haunt me, or maybe just to tell me she is still alive. Not Catherine. The other one.

Hey asshole. Are you sitting in the rain again? Put your dick down, wash your hands, pull up your pants, and give me a call.

He hit return to dial the number. The weak and raspy voice on the other end didn't sound like his friend at first and there was always that moment where Ari experienced the brief surprise that things were really deteriorating.

"That you?" Albert's voice croaks.

"This is me."

"Alright."

"I put it down."

"What?"

"What do you mean what? You told me to put it down and call you, so I did. I don't do that for just anyone."

A rough and whispered chortled rattled on the other end. "Yeah. And did you wash your hands?"

"No. That's where I draw the line and will not be controlled by you or anyone else."

"You're your own man, huh."

"I'm my own man."

"Good for you," the raspy voice suggested before descending into a coughing fit.

"Albert. You OK?"

"Huh?"

"I asked if you were OK."

"Of course I'm not OK."

"That sounded terrible."

"Thank you. Alright then."

"I miss you. How are you?"

"Well. You know, the TV doesn't get ESPN too good, which kind of pisses me off."

"You need to get that fixed."

"You are such a brilliant guy."

"I am."

"Yeah, I got the cable guy coming out. It's not the TV. Probably made the guy's day. Sometimes they actually act apologetic that they can only give me a four hour window when they're gonna arrive. I say no problem, I'll be here."

"Gotta have that ESPN. Were you able to watch the Kings game last night?"

"You should have called me. We could have watched it together and done the commentary together."

"I should have," Ari said, quietly.

"Aren't you almost done with the semester?"

"I taught my last class already. I just have to grade papers."

"Good. Why don't you come out?"

25

"I just might."

"Don't just might. Get your ass on over here."

"My son's leaving the country on Tuesday."

"Simon? It's this Tuesday?"

"Yeah. It's time. So I'm gonna go out and see him before he leaves."

"Wow. I know you probably told me, but now it's happening. That's a big deal my friend."

"He's out to save the world."

"I don't know. At least just see the world. Or part of it. Or *be* a part of it. Good kid. How are you doing with that?"

"What do you mean? I'm proud of him."

"Well. How long will he be gone for?"

"Two years."

"A long time to not see your boy."

"I know that. Yeah. So, that's Tuesday. Maybe I'll see you Wednesday, on the way back."

"Yeah? My dance card is open. I have a doctor's appointment is all." Albert began coughing again, a dry hatchet cough that seemed to last a long time.

"You sound horrible."

"Really? I thought I sounded great." Ari chuckles. "I know. Yesterday I didn't cough very much. Maybe tomorrow will be like that."

"Yeah. So…are you able to work in your garden? Or play your guitar?"

"Not today. You know, only for a few minutes at a time. But I got TV and the internet's an endless distraction. Mostly I sleep."

"Has Gretchen been by?"

"Oh yeah. Every day. She's a good girl."

"Well that's good."

"She only stays a few minutes, though. That's about all that either one of us can stand before she starts to fuss too much."

"Yeah, I guess she fusses to comfort herself."

"She fusses because she's fussy and she's a pain in the ass."

26

"And you love her."

"Of course. I love her to death." He starts coughing again. "Ari, how are you, my friend? Are you staying out of trouble?"

"Afraid so."

"Staying out of the rain?"

"That was just one time." He means the time he sat outside his house for hours, sitting in the pouring rain. Albert had surprised him by coming to see him a bit earlier than expected.

"You stupid son of a bitch. Staying away from your students?"

"That was just one time."

"Staying off the streets?"

Ari sighs. "That was just one time."

"Bull Shit," he hears his friend snigger good-naturedly. "I worry about you sometimes."

"I'm fine. Are you kidding? I love my life here."

"Did you say you're going out to San Jose to see Simon, or is he coming up there?"

"I'm driving out tomorrow morning, first thing. He's having a going away party tomorrow night."

"So you're going to see Sabrina?"

"What is this? The Inquisition? Yeah, I'll see her. I'll probably see that other son of a bitch, too."

"You OK with that?"

"Well I have to be, don't I? I'm an adult and Simon's my son. Right?"

"Well. That's about the size of it, you're right."

"That's about it. I don't have to like it. Especially for Simon's send off."

"No. You don't have to like it. But you probably don't like the fact that he's leaving either."

"Hey. You know. Albert. It just feels a bit like you're trying to figure me out."

"I totally have you figured out."

"Really!"

27

Albert pauses as if he's thinking about this. "Well. Maybe not. You don't have to talk about what's going on with you."

"There's nothing going on with me. Thank you."

"OK. I just find that I'm less and less able to make small talk these days."

And despite the fact that Ari desired to feel nothing but kindness towards his friend, he felt instead something hard impinging heavily in his gut. He wanted to say things he knew he would regret and so he said nothing.

"Don't wait too long before coming to see me, Ari."

"I won't."

Why did Ari disclose his outside relationship with Catherine Lessor? (In the most general possible way.) Could anyone have ever found out? (And found out *what* exactly) Would Catherine have ever said anything? Highly unlikely. Was it guilt? For that other time? Wasn't it just a perverse and ineffective way of covering up what was truly troubling and indictable? Was it to establish his credibility as a man of integrity and thus deflect suspicion away from his real sins?

In fact, Ari had been seen with Catherine at Torinos in Arcata by Cameron and other faculty. Without abashment, Catherine introduced herself, presuming she was easily recognizable anyway. She sang Ari's praises and announced her acceptance to the university. Ari felt himself turn red. Cameron smiled and said in a not unfriendly way that "I'll see you at the office" the next time he was on campus. Nothing was ever said.

Ari had gone to bed, his king size bed, and he opened the window to invite the fog inside. He soon found himself on a wide green valley, well past midnight, a raw starry vault above, tiny little lost figures of people he was sure he knew but couldn't see, running, running, comically, impossibly distant. He didn't know where he was or how he would get home. But he didn't mind at that moment. Over the horizon, a milky sliver of thick fog spilled upon the hills and began to rise and creep upon the plain. He wanted to talk to someone but the only person left was the small, skinny young woman seated in front of him, her face hidden by her short, thick hair. She was looking down, her hands flat in her lap. Face hidden. But Ari knew exactly who she was. And he could guess what she was probably thinking.

So he opened his eyes with relief. The green digital numbers on the clock read 12:37. He looked out and saw that the fog had seemed to lift a bit. Enough to drive. For no reason whatsoever, except perhaps that he was still half dressed, Ari grabbed his car keys.

The fog gave the road the appearance of a tunnel. The turn off to the freeway wasn't so easy to find, even though the road ended just past it. He drove and drove, the fog hugging the road. He could still detect when he neared the ocean, however; the smell, the extra moisture on his arm, the distant crash of the waves against the rocks that he could hear if he slowed his car with the window open.

He didn't think he had intended to drive all the way. He just kept going. Onward, past the beaches and lagoons, into the thick fog of Orick, a desolate hamlet that survived off the trade and production of burls, or polished sculptures from redwood, bears, tables, totems, clocks, and such. Half an hour later, he felt himself pass through the even more modest village of Klamath, to all appearances nothing more than a smoked jerky stand surrounded by emerald fields. Ari reached into his glove compartment to check that his flashlight was still there. He pressed the button and the light reassuringly went on. The fog thickened.

It was only the shift in gravity that suggested he was climbing the hill that meant he was finally getting close to Crescent City. His jaw tightens at the terrible memory.

"Let me get this straight. You're spreading your legs for Paul Langhurst...*and* you're suing *me* for divorce?"

"I'm *asking* you for a divorce. We've moved on from each other already for quite a while, Ari."

"You've consulted a lawyer."

"We can keep this simple. Simon doesn't need any trauma. Neither do I."

"Fine. As long you don't have any trauma... you fucking bitch," he muttered.

"Really, Ari? Do you really want to still be married to me?" Her mind was made up, of course. Was she curious? Incredulous?

Sabrina. Placid. Easygoing. Sensible Sabrina. Deadly. "Or is it that you just can't stand that I made the move, first."

"That's bullshit," he said with force. "Bullshit. And you know it."

"You can say that word as often and as loud as you want, but it still won't make it true."

"Oooh. Put me my in my place," he bit. "That's just insulting, Sabrina."

"You just called me a 'fucking bitch', Ari."

He sighed. Blinked. "I did. I'm pissed and I'm unhappy. An expression of anger. Meaningless. At least I don't mock or dismiss what you say to me."

"Nice rationalizing, Ari. And, oh, 'Bullshit'? That's not dismissive?"

"I was rebutting an outrageous accusation, Sabrina," and he whined in a nasal, mincing voice, "'You're just angry because I made the first move, Ari.'"

"You're not impressing me, Ari. You're mocking me, dismissing me."

"I don't give a fuck about impressing you."

"I know, Ari. You haven't for years."

"Is that what this marriage is about to you? Me impressing you, dancing on my head to impress you…"

"A little attention would….. you know, Ari, I don't want to do this."

He dared to hope she meant the divorce. Of course that's not what she meant at all. "You don't want to do what." He remained standing, hands in his pocket. They had lowered their voices.

"I don't want to argue, and I don't want to tear you down."

"Too late for that. You fucked Paul."

"You're right. It was an ugly thing to do, Ari. It wasn't right. No matter what you might have done in the past. But the marriage was already over. Long over. "

He sighed and shook his head, adjusted his glasses and softly said, "Sabrina. Didn't anyone ever tell you that after you confess to doing something wrong, that you should never follow it with the word, 'But…'"

It was a little before two when Ari pulled into the deepening mists and street lamps of Crescent City. His back felt stiff. He relaxed his hands on the wheel for it had been a long and difficult drive in the fog. He turned away from the wharf into the town's misty interior.

In addition to its notoriety as the Tsunami capital of the pacific northwest, Crescent City, California was also burdened with the highest proportion of child molesters, perhaps in the world. But at least all - or nearly all – were safely incarcerated at nearby Pelican Bay state prison, so that it wasn't really true that the town was pandemic with cannibalism. By day and in sunlight, Crescent City was a decent enough place, though some were poor. But sometimes at this time of night, and in these mists, there was often a strong sense of passing through a graveyard, a despised land where zombies might appear at any moment. The effect added to Ari's sense of excitement and discovery of the occasional streetwalker for sale. There was the time when Ari had slowly cruised K street in the fog, and there suddenly appeared a striking, tall, long legged blond blonde woman, in red shorts, standing still as a post. As he slowly passed her, they locked eyes; her face was wizened, leathery, as frightened as any he had ever seen, large craterous, sunken blue eyes. He had pulled over, his heart pounding, unsure of what he would do. From his rear view mirror, he saw the woman look his way and very slowly step towards him.

There were abandoned and halfway disassembled properties, weeds foaming through cracks in the pavement. Beyond these were a short series of small squalid motels, men with tank tops and tattoos drinking beer and smoking outside. If he dared look their way, they stared right back.

It was in one such sordid place that he had found her that night. His lonely wounded lover. This was all she could afford. Nineteen dollars. First he had spotted her on a bench near the esplanade, looking towards the ocean, but as if she were afraid to walk out on the peer. In the fog, bundled as she was, with a dark woolen cap, even though it was

32

the middle of July, she could have passed for a lank teenaged boy. Most teenaged boys didn't hug themselves when they walked. Ari followed her in his car from what he thought was a safe distance. She was just a scarecrow, a gray mass walking in and out of the fog. Suddenly she quickened her pace and then she was gone.

That was then. Back in December. Now he was back. For no good reason. He creeped along that same street where last he held her. Where last it was that anyone of record bore witness to her. The first motel, the white one, chipped paint, he remembered, paper thin walls. That wasn't it. The yellow one across the way – that was much worse, actual bottles and cans on the brown lawn. That was it. Ari floated to a stop at the curb, pressing in the emergency brake, hearing its reassuring zip, as if the brake could ensure his car would not slide back into the sea or dematerialize in the mist.

He stepped out, the slam of the car door resounding obscenely loud in the forlorn street bog. It was a good guess that merely twenty miles inland that the air bristled instead with the spicy dust of the sunbaked earth, searing at a hundred degrees or hotter. But here instead, at the edge of the world, Crescent City persisted as foggy and fifty four. Here he stood in this beautiful nightmare, forever young, impossibly old, and lost in his shimmering and cloistered slum.

The blast of the car horn shook him from his reverie standing in the middle of the road. A dark late model pick up truck, one of these sleek, monstrous and unnecessary models that Ari loathed and which most owners could barely afford. It rolled slowly by, windows rolled up, menacing rumbles of bass growling, pitch death blackness inside. The truck disappeared into the mists

He looked both ways and crossed. The fog seemed to thin as he stood in the shambled lawn of the motel, imagining that she - that Jasmine was there again, that she had come back and was waiting for him. He would still have to guess which of the tiny, bleak little rooms she was hiding in.

Why was he here? He lived in the most beautiful and comfortable place he could imagine. His own home was a dreamland. Why was he standing here now at this dark place at this dreadful hour? In fairness, Crescent City wasn't so bad. Not really. Strange things happened here once in a while. But it was chilly and foggy in summer, was home to families and children, and within minutes of the Redwoods. Yet it forever wore a purgatorial aspect to it, disappointing, unkind, and neglected.

Heaven lay just to the north in the diffuse comfort of Smith River, then on to Oregon. He'd picked up a gal once in Smith River. Here on this damp tarmac in the cold, there was nothing to do and no one to save. He halfway hoped for an apparition but the only apparition anywhere was himself. He just wanted to sleep, just for a couple of hours. There was a gas station next to the highway. He got himself a large coffee with robust heapings of cream and sugar. Then he entered highway 101 with the relief and chagrin of having duly survived an enormously foolish and dangerous errand. He drove all the way back, 80 miles with the windows down and a loud country western station keeping him company in the dark. With luck, he would be back in his own sanctuary by five - safe – long before the sun caught him out.

But once at home, though greatly relieved, his former restlessness returned and the insane thought occurred to him that he should roll right back again to Crescent City. That's a joke, right? Go to bed! But no, the coffee he had so needed up north had overshot its intended purpose. He was wide awake. Might as well work, he thought.

He virtuously pulled and thumbed through a stack of ungraded papers, a thick sheaf of bland, uninspired, resentful, repetitive, vacuous - why could he not have simply made the whole thing multiple choice? Did he really have to insist on assigning five page papers? Did anyone at all ever give him credit for trying to responsibly teach his students to improve their writing skills, to articulate a cogent, well researched argument, or failing that, a coherent, well written, descriptive sentence. Did Cameron give him any credit at all for 'stepping up' in this way?

Ari prided himself on having enough integrity to challenge his students to learn to write and to think at least a little bit, even though he rarely got better than a high school senior book report. At least everything was typed. But the content was consistently terrible. Sometimes close to half the class flat out ignored his instructions. These people usually got "C"s and should be grateful they weren't summarily failed. A fair number were competent but dull. If they were complete they got at least an A minus. (What a guy I am, he thought.) Ari did not require brilliance and he rarely received it.

By eight o'clock, the day was unusually bright and clear, dry and cool. Ari had powered through most of the papers. There were 64 in all, and he had finished grading 49, managing to stay focused and awake while Stravinsky crashed furiously in the background at three and four and five in the morning. There were no neighbors to object. No one to hear such screams.

He reckoned he barely skimmed the last ten or fifteen papers, mostly checking for key words, the rudiments of sentence structure, the barest hint of a narrative. As daylight brightened, his endurance faded, and his thoughts started to bleed together. How he wanted to be finished already and be done with everything. But he had to lie down. Then again, if I do so, I will end up sleeping right up until he had to get ready to meet this old bag, whoever she was, wherever she was. He would have to stop grading, but Ari had committed to running, every day, and most days that it rained, he ran anyway. So he took a shower to wake himself up, suited up, and stepped outside.

Despite his commitment to run every day, this was his first time in three days. He decided not to let today pass him by lest he fall out of habit. He loved the bracing mists of early morning, the wispy tendrils of fog that receded just beyond his step, the cool wetness that blanketed and isolated every corner, that separated him and his world from the world that belonged to others. More often than not, early morning lasted all day long near Patrick's Point. How he loved the feel of being a satyr like creature in a pretend wilderness, in a charmed forgotten fairy land, void of animal life it seemed. Ensuring his laces were pulled tight, he jogged out from his front door, searching for a narrow dirt road that led to a rarely used fire road, overtaken at turns by wild grasses, dipping fronds, and dripping leaves, gasping in a thin spongy mulch beneath his pounding steps, mesmerizing Ari in its watery breath as he sought after its deepening gloom.

Ari knew that some women found him attractive but he actually thought Sabrina was out of his league. Until they were actually married. She knew how to work, how to plan, how to furnish a home, how to save for something that she really wanted, how to look fabulous. She even knew how to laugh, but rarely it seemed at what Ari found funny. She only laughed at what was obvious, but never what was funny. She couldn't and wouldn't cook, but that was no problem because they both loved to eat out, and Ari himself was the cook, the connoisseur, the seducer, and he cooked for her often when they were first dating. But more or less once they were married, Ari spent little or no time in the kitchen. One day followed another. The relationship felt weightless yet relentless. Though resistant at first to having children, they both felt ready and well equipped to become parents, being stable and safe enough to raise a child in their comfortable San Jose home. From afar he sensed his own fear and angst of the incalculable commitment they were both making, how it begged to command wonder and connection to the earth, but also to something raw and alien, and he managed the sensation with a glass or two of fine red wine, both at lunch and at dinner, as well as by secretly criticizing and judging his erstwhile perfect wife.

Suddenly he slid and fell upon the leaves and skidded down the incline, long before he knew he was actually going down. Once he tumbled, he spun over once on his elbows grasping at mud, leaves, or the root of a tree, his face thwacked when he turned by a bush, his hands and feet splayed, digging at the dirt and smelling the wet and fertile earth. In the shock of that first moment, he wondered if he would be able to get home. He regretted leaving. Maybe I could just sleep right now (and maybe wake up in my recliner chair!) He hated Bud Cameron, as if somehow this were all his fault.

36

There were so many beautiful young women that semester in the Monday night Introduction to Business class. He barely even noticed the awkward, skinny brown girl wearing thick black glasses and barely showing her face through her turned down head. He barely remembered her but for the repeated (and annoying) gesture she had of pushing the square rims of her glasses further up her nose as if she privately feared they would fly from her face at any moment. Her black hair came to her chin and her nose was broad and flat which she made efforts to hide it seemed by looking down and fussing with her glasses. Jasmine somehow refracted energy away from her. She cultivated being invisible. Yet Ari found himself looking at her again and again. And then she was the last person in the room with him. He waited while she walked towards him, looked up and brushed the hair away from her face.

"Yes," he said.

She was looking it seemed at a point several inches to his right. "Um," that was her first word. "Um," that was the second one, too. She pushed her glasses up higher on her face again. Pretty skin, he noticed. "So I'm not like a business major at all. I don't want to take it," she said. "That's just. My deal. But. I have to take this class. I mean. No offense," she said in her stiff, halting, self-conscious way. And she gave out a nervous giggle as if to soften her message. Still she was looking down and to Ari's right.

"OK, " Ari said, non-plussed. What am I supposed to do with that? He smiled and asked, "so how did you get stuck with me then?"

"I told you. I have to take it. It was the only general elective being offered at a time I could take it."

"Really? What's your major?"

"I just started. But I'm planning a double major."

"Which is?..."

"Political science. Environmental science."

Ari suppressed a chuckle. Poli Sci was the biggest bunch of bullshit there ever was. "I'm guessing you'd like to save the earth," he said.

She smiled for the first time, but her eyes were closed, ready to look down. Again she let out her nervous laugh. "Please don't patronize me, Dr. Fisher."

"Mr. Fisher is fine. I'm no Phd."

"Mr. Fisher."

"But it's true, isn't it."

"What's true?"

"You'd like to save planet earth. Or make it a better place."

"Should I make it worse? And are you being cynical about doing good?"

Ari felt himself turning red. "So study business. Seriously."

She made another nervous giggle, standing stiffly, still not seeming to make eye contact, pushing her glasses back up her face. "I see. That's interesting."

"I'm sorry, I didn't catch your name."

She smiled and looked straight at him. "I'm Jasmine," she said, raising a sinewy brown arm and extending her hand. "Pleased to meet you."

Ari mechanically raised his hand and warily took hers. He expected her grip would be weak and non-committal, but he was mistaken. She grasped his hand firmly. He looked at how small her hand felt inside of his.

"So Jasmine. What is it that I could actually do for you?"

"You could give me an A."

"You know you have to earn that."

"Oh I'll earn it. Of course."

"Is that what you wanted to talk about?" Suddenly he realized they were still grasping each other's hand. He let go. She held on for a fraction of a second, long enough for a curious jolt to blink through him.

"Tell me more. What were you starting to say two seconds ago? About why I should take business classes if I want to change the world." And so he told her, putting aside her apparent naiveté and stupidity, and his own incredulity. What was wrong with these young, spoiled, punky students if one could call them that, whose reflex was to cast all business ventures as villainous and rapacious, rather than the source of all her

38

creature comforts, the clothes on her back, the food that she ate, the place where she slept and dwelled in some kind of comfort and security, instead of having to crap in a gutter. He told her the obvious and he told her that the most powerful thing she could do to save the world (whatever conception of hers that involved) would be to apply business acumen and strategy to whatever green or liberal cause that excited her spirit. Stick around. At worst you'll learn something useful. And then, while Ari was still speaking, he suddenly sensed that perhaps this girl was not who she presented herself to be at all. She was smiling. She was smiling and nodding and giggling at a whisper throughout his entire little speech. And the whole time she never once seemed capable of looking at him. But he knew. For reasons he could only guess, the girl was playing him the whole time.

Ari pulled himself into a sitting position and carefully inspected his left ankle, his shins, and his knees, wrists, and hands. He had managed to protect his face as he threw down his hands. Unlike his usual curses at the stubbing of a toe, he had swallowed silent and he sat and tried to assess what shape he was in and what he would do next.

He had scrapes on both his shins and his right wrist. The ankles seemed OK when he rubbed them. The earth was soft and the incline was modest, and Ari was grateful for not having fallen afoul of rocks or other hard and sharp objects. This was truly the wettest and softest spot on the trail. Had he seriously twisted an ankle or broken a bone he might have been hopelessly stuck less than a mile from home for hours or longer. Maybe he would have had to call Bud Fucking Cameron who would have been angry with him for hurting himself and for having to go and take care of this suck-ass woman himself tonight.

Briefly he imagined falling upon unforgiving pavement, upon a sprinkler head, over a rocky incline, his flesh obscenely shredding, years of health, vigor, freedom, pounded senselessly out from his bones and his life. Ari crawled back to the trail and carefully stood, feeling stiff and burning. There was nothing worse than a small trickle of blood upon his right shin. Orienting himself, he slowly began the uncomfortable walk back.

He arrived at his door at quarter past ten, according to his stereo clock. Twice, his feet had started to skid and his knees felt weak. It seemed to take a long, long time as he knew it would. At one point, Ari feared he had somehow gotten off the trail, despite the dozens of times he had traversed it before. Part of him wanted to turn back, to check, but no, he kept going, and just as he was starting to panic, he recognized he was already at the trailhead, less than a hundred yards from his property.

It was ten twenty when he took a shower. Afterwards he sat in his underwear only in his chair. The sun was now unusually bright. A breeze riffled through the trees outside. Then there was silence. Ari felt unusually small in his recliner. He decided to take a bath, a cool one, like his shower to avoid irritating his abrasions. Sitting in silence, feeling too large now for the tub, he lost himself in remembering Jasmine and the time that both of them had wrapped themselves around each other to fit inside each other inside the tub, her face staring strangely impassive, staring through him, her hands on his shoulders, poised to strangle him, just before she throws her head back, exposing her perfect throat...

He tends to his scrapes with antiseptic. At eleven fifteen he makes himself bacon and eggs, toast and coffee. Still, he remembers Jasmine. Eleven forty. His leg still stings and his wrists feel stiff. He mutters, cursing himself softly, then the lousy upkeep of the trail, then himself again, unable to convince himself he can blame anyone else. And he was damn lucky, and he knows it. He puts away the dishes (eleven forty five), putters outside, enjoying the privacy of his own corner of the forest. The fog had been chased away so it was as if time now began again. The sprinklers turned on. Needlessly. He stepped away from the spray. Fog was expected to return late tonight, thicker and more persistent than before.

At noon, Ari decided he had to lie down. He should have been utterly exhausted by now, but instead he felt wide awake and restless, but hollow and tinny; half a moment behind himself, watching himself. If he went to bed now, he could still get four plus hours of solid rest. His cell phone rang on the table inside. Ari walked in and glanced at the number; seeing it was his son, he immediately picked up.

"Hey, buddy," he said in a voice surprisingly loud.

A rich alto came on the line instead of his son. "Hi Ari..."

"Oh. Sabrina?"

"Is this a bad time?"

"A bad time? No. Not really."

"How have you been?"

"Fine. Just fine. Uh...the semester's over. So, just gotta wrap up a little last business and what not. I thought you were Simon calling."

"I know. I hope you're coming tomorrow night to Simon's party."

"Yes...yes, of course," he said, pacing. "He's going away. For a very long time. So of course I'm coming. What do you think?"

"Ari. Easy," she said, and he could see her putting up her hand.

"Please don't tell me 'Easy' -"

"I'm not checking up on you. I was genuinely hoping I would get to see you tomorrow night. "

"I see," he said warily. "Well-"

"And I know how much this means to Simon to see you there."

"Yes.... Simon and I talk."

"You know, Ari, he adores you. He really does."

Ari doesn't say anything, but paces, feeling a distant tightness in her gut. Gently he says, "I hope that doesn't surprise you." Ah! That was a stupid, gratuitous thing to say, he thinks.

"No, Ari. It doesn't. You've always been a good father. I just....I just want you to take that in."

Silence. "Is there anything else, Sabrina?"

"Ari, I called you because I want to tell you something and I want you to hear it from me first."

"Is everybody OK?"

"Everybody's fine. It's very good news. For me.... I'm getting married."

"Oh." His stomach felt cold.

"I guess under the circumstances I don't expect you to congratulate me."

"Congratulations, Sabrina." Ari said stiffly. "Really. I mean, good for you." He wanted to smash Paul Langford's face in with a baseball bat.

"I just wanted you to hear it from me. I didn't want you to be surprised when you came down here."

"Sabrina…that is considerate actually. And as I said before," Ari continued, unwilling to stop himself. "I'm very happy you're marrying the guy you were schtupping while you were married to me. But are you sure you really wanted me to come to the party? I mean it just seems that it would be so much more convenient for you if I didn't come at all."

"Ari. Listen to me please. I did not call to fight. And it's not about me or you. This is about-"

"Paul."

"Simon. Our son. Your son, Simon."

"And his emotional presence. Paul. And his penis, may it reign in glory."

"I was trying to do something decent by calling you."

"Decency would have been much appreciated while we were actually married, darling."

"I'm hanging up."

"Thanks for calling. See you tomorrow." And he shut the phone and shook it, wanting to smash something. Twelve o' five.

Every extremity tingled and throbbed. He felt clenched. This was rage, of course. But he would handle it. What was the point of smashing something he would have to clean up later. (Unless he smashed it and never cleaned it up; unless he just simply lay there in quiet chaos, his own private testament to his futile rage.) Now he was being asked to look at Paul Langford's face without vomiting? He was supposed to congratulate them and smile and even worse watch Paul speak fondly to his own son? His nascent wounds throbbed and burned.

Sabrina was right, of course. This was about Simon, not himself, nor anyone else. But what to do now? Go to sleep? Sabrina had ruined that possibility. Unless, perhaps, he had a drink. And maybe watched a movie. A blue movie, no less. Perhaps. Maybe he could find someone on-line who resembled his ex. No doubt, the male actor would look like Paul, thick set, mustachioed. Good luck.

When Ari eventually told Jasmine all about the dissolution of his marriage, of his cuckold crown, he had no idea how she would react. To his surprise, she winced, eyes half closed. They were sitting together in the mist in the forest on a hike together. She told him, "That sounds so painful."

"Yes. At first," he added.

"You're lying,"

"Lying?"

"It still hurts."

He shrugged. "Well"

"You can tell me. I know the feeling well."

He figured as much. But why did it still hurt? It didn't hurt at all. It just pissed him off. Stay away from my son, you scum sucking insect. Maybe that's why Simon's really going away. To get away from all of us. Ari knew full well he was making everything about him.

Two-thirty. The porn and the booze had definitely taken the edge off. He might have even slept and dreamed through part of it. But he overshot the mark, so to speak, he thought to himself. How lucky am I? Am I not completely free? I can choose to get (mildly) loaded and amped in the middle of Friday afternoon. And in less than 12 hours more, he could do so, if he wished, every day, all summer long. Two-thirty-five. Holy fuck, he had to be there on his little geriatric escort mission at...when? Six o'clock. What if he could only project his more reliable, less interesting avatar to go in his stead so he could stay home and sleep? Three hours until I have to leave, sober, shaved, and dressed.

More relaxed though physically stiff, he had just wasted two hours of precious sleep. But even the two hours that remained to him

43

could make all the difference. First, he decided to check first his phone for a text from his son. None. So he checked his email. On any given day, sitting in front of the computer in his plush leather swivel chair gave him the chance to yawn, to dig his toes in the carpet and relax for a few pointless minutes trolling his emails in the middle of an afternoon, even on a teaching day, much less on the eve of three months of vacation. He felt his back threatening to give away as he rigidly stared at the screen, wagging his heels, eyes popping, lips peeled back from his teeth.

And. No message yet from Simon. There was, however, a message from Bud Cameron. Two forty-three. Fuck. There were two messages, the second having just popped up the moment he looked at the first one. The first - a generic thank you to all the teachers, blah blah. The other one was just for him. But Bud had copied the Abramson. The fucking president of the school.

Thank you, Ari, for stepping up to support the business department at our college. Your efforts are greatly appreciated , demonstrate your commitment to the team, and will considerably help us to seal a much needed investment in our institution, which we all love, which our community depends upon, and of which you an integral part.

So far, so good, he thinks, though it's oddly written and dense. The remark about him being part of the team might have been a partial dig as well, a reminder, a warning. Whatever. A little flowery. Thank you for "stepping up"? Really? Is that professional? Necessary. Thank you for stepping up, you typically self-centered, narcissistic little weed. Thanks. Plus, he's copying Abramson. Really? Did he want to make sure that Ari showed up? Don't trust me? Then he read:

We are counting on you to represent the best of the college. Once again, we appreciate and are grateful for your assistance and discretion in this matter.

44

Don't fuck up, is what it said. Be discreet? Without thinking further, Ari wrote back immediately.

You can count on me.

That's a nice response, he thought. Then he added.

Discretion is my middle name.

His finger hovered over the send button, proud of his little irony. He thought further, imagining Cameron. What was the point? Wasn't it to clearly send him an unnecessary reminder of a commitment he had made the day before? Innocuous and formal. Get over yourself. He sat back in the chair rubbing his chin, his eyes stinging. His knees burned.

Two fifty-one. His head felt light and reeling from lack of sleep. He felt alert yet flyblown. Cameron doesn't trust me. Clearly. OK, so why did he ask you then in the first place? (Yeah, why?) Because he's actually hoping you'll fuck up, buddy (schmuck). That's why. (How could that be true?) Is Paul Langford....or rather Bud Cameron willing to risk a two million dollar deal just to make you look bad? Two fifty-six. It's just a goddamn courtesy note. A thank you! Bud is thanking you. He has confidence in you. He does! Ari went round and round, replaying conversation with his boss in his head, few as they were, imagining things he ought to have said or done or not said or not done, yet the outcome was always the same, the discomfort and dissatisfaction and disappointment, always the same, everything always like a man who drinks water in a dream and is never satisfied. Even when in one such conversation he concludes by smashing Bud Cameron's head through the wall. And now it looks like he'd have to take out the president as well. "I love you, Ari," Cameron says to him. "Relax." Ari opens his eyes, startled, dreaming rapidly at his desk chair.

He peers at the computer screen. Indeed, he had sent his flippant message, and had copied the president as well.

Three-eleven. Ari freely admits he is insane. He smiles. In a moment of clarity he knows for certain that his biggest problem is the racket and the fussing whirling, fogging in his head. He stares out the sliding door. A shadow overhead dims the sun. A cloud. Sadness? Yes. But it's quite simple. He wishes he could somehow just go back to nine or ten o'clock last night, whenever it was that he might have simply gone to bed, even with a night cap and some Nyquil. There was the fog. He wanted to return to the moment when he stupidly, restlessly chose to re-enact his ill-fated chase up to Crescent City. Three-seventeen.

I can still sleep for an hour. That could still help. Better than nothing at all. How he dreaded and resented his little errand. But why? Seriously, Ari admitted to himself. What is the big fucking deal? Really. You take out an old lady, charm her, listen to her, eat some good food, laugh at her jokes, get her home by nine, look the hero, and enjoy your carefree summer hiking and chasing women at every tourist and internet site (except for seventeen ungraded papers and submitting grades by Tuesday noon). Ah, well there was the fact that Simon was leaving. And he would see his son one more time before he left. No matter what. (Fuck you, Sabrina!) Jesus, give it a rest. You live in paradise. You love your life. You created it. You love everything about your little tiny life. I am a spoiled, simpering fool.

Ari walks into his bedroom, mindful of his scrapes and he sets his alarm for 4:30. He undresses, feeling discomfited by the persistent unusual brightness of the day. Fog was predicted for later on.

He closes the blinds and lay down, here on his bed, in the quietest, darkest corner of his remote and soporific lair. The only complaint he'd ever had living here was that unless the wind picked up from the west he rarely heard the ocean, though he lived less than a mile away. That was the only thing he lacked. The entire ocean. And he didn't want that to matter – least of all now – but it did. The awareness of his missing ocean raced ahead and all around him and he knew he would not be able to catch it or contain it. It would do what it would do. The ocean. How he longed to be comforted and reassured by its presence, the nearness of this infinite living being.

46

The shore was that place, the edge, that simple, uncultivatable last few inches which ended where a mystery began. The sand at Patrick's Point was coarse and uninviting, covered in driftwood. Nine days out of ten, it was cold and windy and the ocean and the sky were the color of metal. What could be more caressing than to hear it, nor more terrifying than to be lost inside of it? Regardless of his landlubber ignorance, the ocean forever exists, infinitely more real than himself, the ocean, teeming with worlds and unspeakable creatures and infinite loneliness. All he asks is for the chimera of its distant caress. Instead, he lies awake, eyes burning yet bolt opened, unable to hear, feel, or sense it. Nor even imagine it. No edge. No mystery. No ocean. There was only an airless stillness, a forlorn, neglectful quiet. Give it a rest. Rest! Sleep. He thought of taking the Nyquil, but knew that would be foolish right here, right now. Surely he would overshoot the mark. It was now three-thirty-four.

Fifty-six minutes until he had to get going if he was going to be clean, dressed, and on-time. Not a moment of precious sleep in the last 36 hours (but for a few minutes of hallucinatory limbo) and he had just 56 minutes to make up for it. And it was too goddamn quiet to sleep! Jasmine was looking down as he let himself in, sitting while staring at the back of her hands in her lap. Strange to say, she had not locked the door.

He opens his eyes, his chest heavy. Asleep? Three-forty. Six minutes of sleep but he dared not go back to sleep. Not if she was waiting for him. Not if he were stuck back in that room. He felt restless and airless and an odd and unaccountable sensation of being tucked away on a shelf, a feeling of being put aside by nothing at all in his own home.

Ari rises and takes a long, mild shower, his second of the day. He had to mind his scrapes lest he fiercely aggravate them. Ari shaved, washed his hair, slowly dried, and applied deodorant, extra for some reason, and what he considered a light dash of aftershave. The cool shower revives him immensely, and with the hour of dread at hand, he feels his confidence returning. He makes himself a double cappuccino and grabbed a bottle of water. Carefully, he chooses an outfit as if preparing for an anticipated date instead of a tedious and inconvenient errand. He stands in his kitchen and sips his coffee which is already cooling. He gulps the rest, not too hot, brushes his teeth, and adorns his silk shirt and sport coat. I am ready for "stepping up."

But before leaving he padded for moments throughout the house, anxious that he was forgetting something. Keys? Wallet? Phone? He enters his bedroom again and stands there. The bed had barely been disturbed. Though it wasn't his habit to make his own bed every day, today he straightened it out. So it would be ready for him? He takes a last look around as if this were the last time he would see this quiet place in quite a while. Ready to go.

Ari was bound to get to the hotel very early after all. Cameron would be proud of him! Maybe he'd treat himself to a drink or two first at the hotel bar. Four-eighteen. By nine or nine-thirty at the latest, he would be back home in bed ready to sleep a good twelve or thirteen hours before leaving to his see his son. He should certainly be well rested for that. Ari felt gratefully alert. Get in. Get out. Four nineteen and he walked out of his bedroom, picked his keys up from their place, and walked out the door.

The drive was uneventful except for light traffic into Arcata. The airport with its one runway was in a sweet grassy clearing surrounded by trees in the middle distance. The Comfort Suites stands alone near one end of the field, a three star hotel with a long drive way, looping its way from the 101. The day was so amazingly clear that it was difficult to believe that a thick marine layer was expected to penetrate its way inland within a few short hours.

Where was he supposed to meet this goddamned Mrs. Ng? He could always have the front desk ring her room. But he was actually early, so Ari entered the bar which was empty, how he liked it, except for the irritating "soft jazz" - a euphemism he felt for desultory pop sputum laced with sophomore saxophone play. There was also a news show tinning on the television. Five oh five.

Incredibly, he was nearly an hour early. I am a professional is what I is. Ari smiles at the young blonde who serves him his vodka tonic. She gives him the most scant and obligatory hints of a smile. He nods, opens his tab and takes his drink to a table in the lobby, realizing how foolhardy it was for him to drink on an empty stomach and a day and a half with no sleep. But apart from a little boredom and a little soreness, Ari feels well. The drink would amuse him. He settles in further, congratulating himself. The front desk was empty. Dissonance from the bar - from the TV and the piped music – was barely out of earshot. He puts the drink down, closes his eyes, sure that it was only for the briefest of moments. The last thing he remembered was that he meant to call Simon.

Ari opens his eyes. For a weird and frightful moment, Ari has no sense at all of where he is. He remembers. What time is it? Ari straightens, rubs his temples, and suddenly worries about whether he has made himself the fool by snoring or drooling in a public place. He gives himself a once over his face, nose, and mouth, checking for indiscretions. Everything's fine. Ari stands, straightens his coat, his hair. Rubbing his glasses with a stray piece of crumbled, unused facial tissue, Ari looks out and starts violently, astonished to see for the first time, someone sitting in the chair a coffee table's distance away. Already he is certain he knows who it is.

Putting on his glasses, the blur resolves itself as a tiny woman, dressed in a bright red silk top, white slacks, and a large red cap and tight little sunglasses that lent themselves to the effect that there were dark holes in her head where her eyes should have been. A cold foam of shame whistles through his belly. She crosses her legs, upper foot rocking up and down.

"Hello," he blurts, feeling self-conscious and resentful. "Can you tell me what time it is?" he says, feeling stupid, pretending she was no one in particular.

Mrs. Ng smiles. Small as a child, fiercely dark, hair braided in vicious, flailing corn rows, she smiled, large straight white teeth radiating from excessively thick lips. In a voice deeper than he expects, with perfect elocution, she tells him, without glancing at her watch, "Why it's only 5:37." She leans back in her seat, dangling a little hand near her head, a lazy yet studied gesture.

"Thank you," Ari says.

"Why no. Thank you, Mr. Fisher," she replies. "I'm quite flattered that you actually arrived so early. You must have been looking forward to this as much as I have." And for a flash, Ari thought he saw her smile suddenly fade. But now it was back.

He allows himself a chuckle. "Ari Fisher, yes," he says. "Very nice to meet you, Mrs. Ng." He notices feeling strangely distant from himself, as if he were remembering or watching this very moment, instead of living it. There he is, extending his hand, but there was the table between them, so he comes around instead to offer it. Mrs. Ng looks at it and for one shrill moment, Ari imagines she will not take it. Now she looks up at him, sweeps her glasses from her forehead, revealing her jet black eyes, and she puts her long, thin, tiny hand firmly in his gripping it with surprising strength. "Mr. Fisher," she says, flashing her sharp incisors towards him. She wore large golden bracelets around her narrow wrists. "So," she says, tilting her head. "It seems you are the one stuck with me tonight."

"Hmm? Ah. No. I'm delighted and honored to meet you. It's a pleasure," he lies. "We are so indebted to you," he says, scanning his tone for hints of irony. "The least we can do is be good hosts." She says nothing, nods. "So," Ari continues. "I thought I'd tell you that I plan on taking you to our finest restaurant, a beautiful place called Turendotte, right in the middle of the forest."

"I'm sure it's wonderful."

"And then….if you're up for it, we can catch a night cap at a place right up on the water in Trinidad."

"A pleasure."

"Our reservations are for six thirty. But we have a few minutes…if you want to get a drink."

"Why don't you sit down?"

"Alright." And he sits down next to her. He realizes he is still holding her hand. He lets go.

"I don't know if he told you, but…well, I asked for your personally, Mr. Fisher."

"You did?" Ari feigns surprise. "Tell me."

50

"You were my grandson's favorite instructor. So I wanted to meet you. Because of Leon."

"Leon?"

"Yes. You must know I had a grandson who went to your school."

"Yes, of course. What a tragedy."

"Don't you remember him?"

"Yes, I'm sure that I do." He doesn't. "Leon. Leon Ng," he says, to buy more time. Not good. Mrs. Ng nods and smiles, eyes narrowing, lips pursed, but appearing as if her teeth might burst through at any moment. "Well," Ari continues. "Of course. I know the name well from the papers. But," he confesses. "I'm not so good with associating names with faces in my classes. I do apologize." Ari feels himself sweating, appalled with his dismal inability to dissemble well.

She cocks her head and raises an eyebrow. "Of course, Mr. Fisher. Of course. I should not be disappointed. You have hundreds of students. Many hundreds. But you need to know that you made a distinct impression on him."

"Ah," Ari scans an empty landscape for something to say to this. I'm fucking up, he thinks. How could this be so difficult? Suddenly he realizes he should simply ask her to tell him more. "Please....perhaps you would tell me more about Leon."

"You are truly so lucky to live in such a beautiful, magnificent place," she breaks in, dismissively.

"It is beautiful!" he smiles, feeling his voice break out, loudly. "It is heaven. I love it." I am an idiot, he thinks. An idiot! "But it also must be so different, I imagine, from Vietnam."

"I live in south San Francisco, Mr. Fisher," she corrects him with perfect congeniality.

"Ah. Yes. For some reason I thought you were originally from Vietnam."

"And so I am. Originally. But I've lived her now in California for forty-five years. How is my English, Mr. Fisher?"

"Better than mine, actually."

She smiles, devastating her face with sudden, subversive lines. "Shall we go to your restaurant? We can have a drink there if we arrive early."

He could think of nothing to say or that he wanted to say and his discomfort mounted. Glancing at her, she looked as stony silent as a statue, watching the forest passing by. Turendotte's was the one truly high end restaurant in all of Humboldt county, courting a muted, somber elegance, dark wood and leather, shimmering pea green walls, prints of stills and sunken abstract expressionist paintings, gold and rust and flame and black. As if seeing it for the first time, Ari was appalled by its heavy, ponderous, oily airs. The evening was already taking forever.

"How long have you lived up here, Mr. Fisher?"

Small talk. Good. "It will be four years this September."

"Ah. You know exactly. And you love it?"

"I do," Ari said truthfully, aware of a cold echo of sadness. "I really do."

"Well, what brought you here? I take it you're not from around here."

"Correct. My family, we moved out here when I was ten from Ohio to San Jose where I'd lived until moving here."

"And so what then brought you here? I suppose I could guess."

"Well, it was the school. I found a wonderful home here at the college."

"Yes, of course. And what else then? The beauty?"

"Of course."

"The forest. The sea."

"Yes. And yes."

"The peace and quiet."

"Right again."

"The loneliness."

"Excuse me?"

"Yes. The loneliness. This is a beautiful, but desolate place, to tell the truth. And you like that well enough, Mr. Fisher."

"And why do you say that, Mrs. Ng?"

52

"I'm just very intuitive. I'm good at reading people. I've had to be."

"You're saying that I like being lonely?"

She smiles, her large teeth jumbling into view. The sight of her teeth somehow made her seem more vulnerable than menacing. "An odd thing to venture to say, I grant you. I believe I see pain trapped in your gaze, Mr. Fisher."

"Mrs. Ng. Do you suppose we could call each other by our first names, if we're going to look into each other's souls tonight?"

"I'm not a formal person, Mr. Fisher. And I'm not here, it's true, to talk business with you, at least not where the school is concerned. It's just that it seemed like it would be most…stimulating, I think, for us to *earn* that kind of familiarity with each other tonight," she said slowly. "What do you think?"

"What do I think?" Ari felt light headed. Mrs. Ng had ordered some sort of pink drink, the color of neon grapefruit, which she had not even touched. He felt faintly nauseous looking at beads of condensation slowing sinking down the rim of her oversized glass. He himself was half way through his vodka martini. Already, he had forgotten if this was his first or second, since arriving. He allowed himself to stare into Mrs. Ng's singular face; chiseled dark, tightly wound skin for a woman perhaps in her sixties. Her opaque and impervious eyes contrasted with the sunken quality in which her sockets sat deep within her face, giving it a mildly panicked expression of which her eyes were quite oblivious.

"You're suggesting that we see if we might somehow before the end of this evening, that we might get to know each other well enough, or connect well enough so that we really and truly earned the right to call each other by our first names. Does that sound like what you are suggesting?"

She smiled and narrowed her eyes. "Yes…Mr. Fisher."

"It's as if," he pursued, "somehow being on a first name basis would be well, intimate in a way. Almost taboo."

"Very good, Mr. Fisher. Very good. Taboo. Forbidden, yes. That's a fun game to play, I should think."

"Very well, Mrs. Ng. Very well. So be it."

"So be it, Mr. Fisher."

"I hope you're hungry, Mrs. Ng."

"Always, Mr. Fisher."

They reviewed the menus in silence. The waiter came and went with their orders. To his amazement, she ordered the steak and lobster. He smiled, imagining she wanted to earn back part of the two million dollars she donated. Not in cash, but in some kind of estate funding deal. But there was no way she could actually steak and lobster. Ari ordered the salmon. They would share a bottle of Chianti. Somehow the salmon, he realized, would conservatively compensate for other choices he had already made this evening, or was about to make.

"Mrs. Ng," he said, enjoying the childish sound of her name on his lips. He considered he should probably lay off the vodka.

"Mr. Fisher," she said. Ari considered simply repeating 'Mrs. Ng' and hearing 'Mr. Fisher' in return, ad infinitum, iterating a trance like, stupid dyad, riling one another up. And with that the conversation finally lightened and buoyed, skimming like polished stones across the mist rimed waters, disappearing without a sound. Yet there were always more such stones at hand. Mrs. Ng talked about opera. She had been both a singer herself as well as an avid fan; opera, modern art, and transcendental meditation. Ari was able to contribute with anecdotes about the weather system, the Redwoods, and the essential role of mist and fog. Mrs. Ng leaned forward attentively. Sailing, hiking, the evolution of streams and rivers; he made the most of these as they skimmed their lovely stones into the mist. Salad and soup arrived.

Ari, feeling affable, buttered his bread and said in a voice louder than he intended, "This is delightful, Mrs. Ng. You have been so good to us. It's extraordinary."

She leans forward, "Let's then talk about that. I did it to remember, my grandson. I did it because I have plenty of money to give away, Mr. Fisher, and perhaps not so much time to spend it."

"I see."

"Do you?"

"No, of course not. How could I really know? I've never done such a thing."

"I'm not going to live forever. None of us will. But honestly, I feel like I already have. I have been preparing myself for some time now. Any moment, the next moment itself, could be my last, my demise."

"What are you talking about?"

"Heart attack. I've already had three. All of them small. I pushed right through them. It started with fever and heartache as a child. The next time may be quite different. My end is likely to be swift and sudden."

"Wow. You're like a time bomb, Mrs. Ng. But that's not a bad way to go, is it?"

"Is it? No chance to say good-bye?"

"You'd have to be prepared."

"I suppose it could work if I could choose the moment."

"And what moment would you choose?"

She narrowed her look at him. "Even if I knew such a thing, I don't think I would tell it to you, Mr. Fisher."

"Very well. Then I hope you live a very long time."

"I already have, Mr. Fisher."

"It doesn't show, if that's the case. Would you like anything else to drink?"

"I haven't finished with the one I have."

"Your glass is half empty. I'll order us another."

"Reckless, are we?"

"It's the boss's dime."

"As you wish. Drink up, Mr. Fisher. Just be ready."

The main courses arrived. Mrs. Ng's plate seemed absurdly large. "Please, Mr. Fisher. Yes? You like to consume. I can tell you are a man of voracious appetites. The salmon will not be enough for you. You shall devour much, much more than that this evening." And so she heaped significant portions of her steak and lobster onto his plate, succulent and bursting. He began to amaze himself with ease and

55

comfort with large portions of aggressive food, replenished alcohol, and virtually no sleep. Ari felt momentarily indestructible and dangerous. He was feeling very, very good, light weight and not in the least bit bored.

Time must have passed. Ari could not say how much. He blinked his eyes and looked around assuring himself he was wide awake and completely present. Suddenly he wonders whether he had not blacked out at some point, if only for a moment, or whether even now he was in fact, still dreaming, still haunting another dimension. Mrs. Ng's plate and his own were now empty, abandon of food, nothing but the juices of beasts. She seems to be answering a question that he could not recall asking.

"Our lives, Mr. Fisher, so often pivot on decisions we make or have already made at critical moments in our lives. Don't you think?" Ari considered this to be the most obvious notion in the world, but he says nothing. He nods a great deal. She continues. "Freedom isn't endless. You can only stand at the same fork in the same road so many times. Maybe only once."

"When you bathe in a river, it is never the same river as the one you bathed in before" Ari offers. "Never the same water," he needlessly clarifies.

Mrs. Ng shrugs and looks off, as if impatient with Ari's misguided attempt to improve upon her own analogy. "Yes. I suppose. That's not quite apt, but…. But sometimes those pivotal moments, they come and they go and they simply pass us by as if we were asleep the entire time, sleeping so sweetly in our lovely blanket of mist." She smiles at him and winks. Ari wishes he was in his own bed right now, regretting how he spurned his own chances at sleep and quiet. "Nevertheless, Mr. Fisher," whether asleep or awake, we make our decisions; we seal our fates just as surely at those moments of such sleep as at any other moment. From then on the decisions we make are as if they have already been made for us, for we can no longer truly decide otherwise than to choose poorly. And the reason we fail to choose wisely is because we have long ago already chosen to walk down a dead end path. Try as we might, when it now comes time to decide, it is as if we are destined forever more….to act the fool. Some people act the fool, Mr. Fisher. And because they cannot do otherwise, they continue to act that until they finally arrive at their incontrovertible dead end, unable to turn back." Ari was sure that even Mrs. Ng had very little idea of what she was talking about. He just smiles and nods. Then she looks directly at him and with sudden vehemence, her eyes flashing, she announces, "That's not how I've lived my life, Mr. Fisher. I make my choices and I live with them. I'm no fool." Her face is like a stone but then she softens and a smile breaks out and she cocks her head and touches his wrist. "I was quite emphatic just now, wasn't I?"

"That's quite alright."

"Yes. It is. Are you enjoying your meal, Mr. Fisher?"

"Tremendously," Ari affirms, sopping up his sauce with a dinner roll.

"Impressive, Mr. Fisher."

Ari smiles. He wipes his face with a napkin, searching out any accusatory dribble from his lips or chin. None. Mrs. Ng continues:

"Leon was not the only child of mine - grandchild, of course - who was a student of your university. Of your college, I should really say." "It's a pity you don't remember him better." I mean, of course, you have so many children, you cannot be expected to remember them all. But he remembered you. He spoke of you to me."

"He did?"

"Yes. And so did-"

"I remember him!" he said.

For a moment, her face seemed to sag into the folds of disappointment. But then she brightened and smiled, her black eyes impassive, an impression of a gracious and appreciative nod. "Well then. What do you remember?"

During an actual midterm, Ari had no choice but to proctor his own exams. He spent most of his time behind his laptop at the front table, resembling someone who might be working but who was instead, surfing the internet idly considering the purchase of books and music.

He had typed in the name of one singer in particular considering her music a guilty pleasure. Ari created a separate search for her, scanning her images. The woman was ferociously beautiful. Excessively lovely in her first youth yet quickly eroding, darkness corrupting her features, her exquisite eyes now burning and haunted, repulsive with pain more moving to Ari than ever.

Guiltily, he exited both tabs and he peered over the monitor to view the squirming mass of students struggling through his mid-term. This one was multiple choice, scantron, easy to grade. Ari glanced at the tops of student's heads, until his attention was trapped by the quiet face of a young Asian male student, staring intently, pencil in hand, at the scantron of the young woman directly in front of him. Ari stared at the boy who glanced up at him. Their eyes met.

Time was up and the students were filing rapidly out of the classroom, some of them with defeated looks on their faces, others with an affectation of utter forgetfulness. "Son, I need to talk to you for a minute." Ari rarely addressed his students with such affectionate condescension as 'son'.

"Yes, sir." Ari and Leon faced each other, eyes averted, while the others drained away. Ari closed the door.

"Sit down. Please." The boy sat without the least show of curiosity. He sat looking at his hands. Ari guessed that he knew why he was here. He pulled his chair around in front of his table so he could sit next to him instead of across from him. "I'm sorry. I can't remember your name."

The boy looked up. "It's Leon, sir. Leon Ng."

"Leon. OK. We haven't spoken much this semester, so forgive me. Anyway. Do you know….do you know, perhaps, why I asked to speak to you, just now?" The boy's eyes seemed to flutter. He rubbed the sides of his jeans in his thighs. Ari suspected the boy did not even know he was doing this. But it still annoyed him. "What do you think, son?" Ari sat back.

Leon looked up and nodded. Looked down again.

"You know, Leon, you've just put me…well, yourself mostly, in a very awkward position. You realize that."

"Yes."

"Look, maybe we can work something out. That's possible. But I want you to level with me. Look at me, son." Leon looks up, emotion slowly emerging. He maintains his eye contact with Ari. "I want to see what I can do here. But I want you to tell me the truth."

"Yes sir."

"Is this your exam right here?" Ari held up the scantron between two fingers, as if he did not really care to touch it much.

Leon squinted. "Yes. Yes sir."

"Leon, I sat here at my desk and watched for twenty minutes while you stared at the scantron of the student sitting right in front of you. Followed by copying down her answers."

"Oh. Yes. I did that."

"Why?" Ari blurted out. "I mean, I don't get it. I've never seen anything like it."

The boy pushed his glasses higher on his face. "I'm sorry."

"How do you even know that this girl knows what she's doing any better than you? Or that I didn't give different tests to different people. I mean, those are the least of my questions."

"I'm very sorry."

"So you admit you were trying to cheat."

"Yes sir."

"Alright....I remember your paper now. It was very good. Exceptional. Did you write it?"

"Yes sir."

"Do you understand that you're risking at the very least a failing grade in this class?"

"I....I guess. Yes sir."

Ari rocked in his chair and scratched at something on his shoe. He sat up again. "What do you think we should do? I'm serious. I'm not sure."

"I get really nervous. I don't like exams."

"Really. Did you take the SAT? I hear it's hard to cheat on that. They even have essays"

"Yes."

"Do you remember how you did?" Leon told him. Ari raised an eye brow. "Well if that's so, what are you doing in this cow patch? You should be at Humboldt. At least."

"My grades weren't very good."

"I don't get it."

"I had a lot of distractions back then. I guess."

"Alright. I'll tell you what," Ari put his hands together. "Tomorrow afternoon at four o'clock, I want to see you right here in this classroom. I happen to know it's not in use."

"What are you going to do?"

"Here's what *you're* going to do. You're going to take the same exam all over again. All by yourself. You will bring nothing but a pen and a pencil. You'll have the same amount of time as tonight. But I'm also giving you three short essay questions. I'm not even going to take points off the exam. Your score will be your score. The essay questions should be balance enough. Understand."

"I....I...thank you. But I....I have to work. I'm sorry."

"Bullshit, Leon. You'll call in sick on your job and you *will* be here tomorrow at four. Trust me, you will not like the alternative. Are we clear?"

Leon stared at Ari with his mouth. "Yes sir."

"You'll be here."

"Yes sir."

"What time?"

"Four o'clock."

"And if I ever see or even hear about you cheating again in mine or anybody else's class at this school, I will see to it that our academic dishonesty policy is rigorously enforced, which will mean, 'bye-bye'. Got it?"

"Of course, I remember now. He had come to see me several times while taking a finance class with me. A nice, quiet, respectful young man. Smart, too, and…. hard working. I hope I helped him a little bit while he was with me."

"Undoubtedly," she said, rather dismissively. "And thank you for remembering him," she said more softly.

"Again, I know it sounds so inadequate, but I'm very sorry for your loss."

"My loss is your gain. Isn't it?" She winks at him, no doubt referring to her donation to the school.

What an ugly, uncalled for thing to say. Ari is sure he dislikes her. Stiffly he tells her, "The world would be more restored without your money in our school and with your grandson still alive and well."

"I agree, Mr. Fisher. It would be far better if both my grandchildren from your school were still with me."

"Both your grandchildren?"

"Of course. Leon's cousin. His little cousin. No one's heard from her in months. She has apparently disappeared."

"My god. That's terrible."

"Of course. Perhaps you remember my granddaughter?"

Ari felt a dread, a tangled web of black adrenalin spurting through his viscera. "Perhaps. Who was she?"

"You mean who *is* she?"

"Excuse me?"

"Who is she? You spoke of Jasmine in the past tense."

Ari sits back. There it is. Jasmine. He closes his eyes and opens them again. "I did?"

"You said, 'who *was* she'. Pay attention, my good Mr. Fisher."

"Of course. I'm terribly sorry. I was thinking of her only as a student of ours in the past tense. For now."

"I might wonder what you were thinking."

"Jasmine Ng?"

"Her father's name is Ramirez. Jasmine Ramirez. Don't worry. I believe she is wandering out there, somewhere, very much alive. And that she will in time return to us. To me. Do you remember her?"

Ari realizes there is no advantage and every risk to deny that he does. "Of course, I do. Yes, she was a student of mine," he offers,

61

feeling himself innocent in his boldness. "I remember Jasmine. Hard not to." After all, I knew every sweaty, honey colored inch of her.

"What do you remember, Mr. Fisher?"

"What do I remember?" He remembers her animal smell, her hot breath in his ear and upon his neck.

"Yes, I'm glad of it. What do you remember? Tell me now. What do you remember of my granddaughter?"

"She stood out. I remember....I remember, she approached me the first day of her first class, and she told me she was uncomfortable with taking business classes. I worked with her a little bit on this. I suppose she was idealistic."

Mrs. Ng laughed out loud, an odd choppy, whiny cascade. "Did she now? Did she tell you she was uncomfortable with business?"

Ari smiled, only because Mrs. Ng was smiling. "Like she was uncomfortable with the idea. As if somehow, it was almost fascistic and imperialistic to even learn anything about capitalism. But she was a bright girl. *Is* a very bright girl. Exceptionally so. Maybe a bit naïve." Maybe he had already said too much, critiquing her runaway, sullied granddaughter, cousin to her dead and rotting grandson.

"Did Jasmine ever tell you that when she stayed with me, that at the age of six, she used to steal my jewelry and try to sell it openly on our street corner? Later, she actually started a lemonade stand, with lemons stolen from a neighbor's tree."

"Really. She was very energetic. As a young girl."

"There's your little socialist for you, Mr. Fisher."

"How about that."

"How about that, yes. So Mr. Fisher. What did you think of my granddaughter?"

"Oh....you mean beyond what I just told you?"

"What was she like? You've only told me some farce she told you about her aversion to business." Ari remembers clearly that the subject had never more surfaced at any time between after that very first conversation.

Ari grits his teeth. "Well, I didn't know here well, of course," he lied. "She seemed....rather nervous and insecure. Yet, rather bold and

62

determined; she was….she always seemed shy and quiet, but very passionate and feeling. I guess a bit of a paradox, your granddaughter"

"Passionate! You found Jasmine passionate, you say," Mrs. Ng pursued.

"Yes," Ari admits, feeling himself redden. "What I mean is…she attached to certain ideas, as young people often do, and she seemed fond of arguing them regardless of her grasp upon the relevant facts."

"That just sounds foolish, I'm afraid, to do that. But maybe that is Jasmine, after all."

"It's actually not such a bad trait for a young person. But I mean, she asked lots of questions and was willing to learn. To challenge your boundaries, to test your environment. There's nothing wrong with that."

"What kinds of questions did she ask you, Mr. Fisher? If you can remember."

"Why did you get divorced?" she called over her shoulder with a grin. He struggled to keep up with her. Jasmine's movements were easy and fluid, unconstrained it seemed by the tightness of her jeans. Ari liked to watch her from behind, but he felt resentfully old as he labored up the trail with her, an avenue of mists, mossy green lichens and ferns hugging the footpaths. A tumorous growth of coral colored mushrooms the size of a dead dog exploded into view on his right.

"I told you before. She was sleeping with another man." His voice sounded absurdly loud banging against the towering Redwoods. "Why do you keep asking me?"

"Well something led to that, didn't it?" She turned her head and was smirking at him, it seemed.

"Can we not talk about this while we're scaling this hillside?" he puffed.

"We'll find our place to sit and eat. And we can talk it about it there!"

63

"I can hardly wait." She suddenly galloped ahead, giggling, taunting. Jasmine disappears around a curve, fingers of fog swelling into the void. For a cold moment, he fears he won't be able to find her.

They ate their sandwiches in the damp and blackened hollow of a two-headed behemoth of a tree set back a few feet from a level part of the trail. She asked him, "How can you wear just a pair of shorts and a tee shirt?"

"I'm quite comfortable."

" 'I'm quite comfortable'" she intones in her pseudo stern tenor, frowning and tucking her chin. "You're not cold, are you." It wasn't a question.

"I still have the shirt here tied around my waist, in case I do get cold."

"But you're not cold."

"No. I'm not. Are you?"

"I'm cold."

"Even in jeans and a sweatshirt."

"Even so." And she moved up close to him.

"You like it warm."

"I like it hot."

"Why didn't you move to Redding? Or somewhere else warmer."

"Because I get my crappy education paid for here."

"Interesting choice of words."

"So why did you get divorced?"

He chewed and leaned back. "To be honest, maybe the real question is, how did we stay together as long as we did?"

"So what kept you together as long as you were?"

"Why do you want to know?"

"Why do you think? Because I want to know you. I think maybe you and I are more like than you think."

"How so?"

"You answer my question first. About how you stayed together as long as you did."

"I'm not so sure we're at all alike, Jasmine. Maybe that's what's interesting."

"We are alike. I think that's what draws me to you," she says as if deciding, Ari thinks, what kind of cereal she prefers.

"How are we alike? I'm a divorced white dad over 50. You're a teenaged Asian girl."

"First of all, I'm American. Second, that's boring, what you just said. Do you really think I'm that stupid?" But she's running her hand through his hair as she says this.

He pulls away, regretting doing so. "You are anything but stupid. Reckless, maybe. Feckless."

"Inscrutable, perhaps?" and she pulled with each forefinger against the shape of her eyes, as if to imitate the Asian she already was.

"OK. You're right. I'm being extremely boring. So how are we alike, my dear?"

"What do you think?"

"Smart? Rebellious? Sassy? Incredibly good looking."

"Lonely." She looks at him and gives a mild shrug. "Both of us. We're both alone. And we're both lonely. Very….lonely. Right?"

Ari pauses. "I was going to disagree. But…"

"But that would be boring, Ari. What would be the point of that?"

"I've never actually known anyone like you, Jasmine."

She smiles. "Except yourself, right?"

"I don't know about that. And loneliness is hardly the cement for a relationship."

Her eyes widen. "Relationship?"

"Friendship. Arrangement," he returned. They had not yet slept together. Ari was on fire, yet wondering if he should have his head examined. Her talk of loneliness chilled him, gave their outing the pall of a dark, wounded arc through which they inexorably trudged, as if their anticipated mating was about to be forged in blood. They had kissed but one time. In of all places, his car.

"I know. Whatever it is that makes us alike. It'll turn us against each other."

65

"Maybe. Do you want an apple?" Mango is more like it, he thought, thinking of her hot and humid mouth. She was like a spicy ripe fruit. He knew it would be 'extremely boring' to her if he told her that. Racist too, perhaps, but it was the boring part that would annoy her.

"No thanks. So, why do you think the marriage lasted as long as it did?"

He settles back against the tree and lets out a muffled laugh. "Well... my ex is beautiful. We got along fine. And...I was probably just oblivious that anything was wrong."

"I can believe that."

"You can?"

"Yes. Oblivious sounds like you. You like oblivion. Love it."

"What the hell, Jasmine."

"Continue. Please continue. What else."

"What else kept us together?"

"Yeah."

"My son. Our son."

"Ah. *Simon*."

"Simon."

"You stayed with her because of him?"

"Well...it's more like it never occurred to me that the marriage could end. Because of him."

"You love your boy."

"Yes," Ari said simply.

"More than anyone?"

"Yes. That's right."

"I believe you."

"Good."

"I like that about you."

"He's a good kid. He's....he's a good man."

"Like his father," she asked, arching a brow.

"Oh god, better than that. Much. Better."

"How old is he?"

"I told you before. Twenty two."

She giggles and sidles up closer to him. "Twenty...two. So. Do you think I'd like Simon?"

Ari chuckles softly. "You stay away from Simon. He's a nice boy, I told you."

"Do you think Simon would like me?" Here she smiled broadly, pleased with herself, it seemed. Her teeth were yellow and sharp. She was odd looking. Her skin was perfect. Her body seemed to vibrate. Purr. She twisted her body towards him. Slinky savage.

"So...." she said. "Little boy, Simon, is twenty...two. Yes?"

"Yes, he is. He's a big boy."

"Well. He'd be just right for me." She eased in closer. "A nice...older...man" And she licked Ari on the mouth, her eyes, always half shut it seemed, rolling in her head. Ari held her face, watching his crude fingers, hairy knuckles, against her flawless skin; he was a pentapod, straining stiffly against his slacks, a carnivore, predator, a hairy beast with claws, willing to devour her, bones and all. But he also had to shake away the conjured image of his blameless boy, a strange splice, loops of feigned desire between young lovers, she and Simon, forbidden to aging, lumpy silverbacks like Ari Fisher. She rolled softly in his palms, eyes fluttering, then smiled, fleshly lips smacking and she shook her head and withdrew, taking his ogre like hands in her own little ones, buttery brown, dainty but for her ravaged cuticles and jagged fingernails. "I'm not done with you, yet."

"Yes? Tell me."

"I have more questions."

"Oh, God," he said, but he was smirking, and he decided he didn't care. They were in a timeless place. No school. No one for miles. What if some students came along hiking? Cameron? The mists closed off the trail that brought them here. Ari relaxed, as if the fog and mist had settled the matter.

"I can't remember the specific questions she asked, but they always demonstrated a careful reading and a vivid interest in the topic."

"I see. Was she a good student?"

67

"Very. I mean she's brilliant. An agile mind. But, she didn't turn in her final assignment, so I had to give her a 'C'," he said, wondering why he couldn't have simply given her a one word answer and left it at that.

"Just like her. How unnecessary!" Mrs. Ng blurted. "Utterly feckless." At least she never cheated on an exam, Ari thinks. As if reading his mind, Mrs. Ng observes.

"Poor Leon. He drove his car over the rocks in your wretched fog."

"Horrible."

"Yes. And what's worse is that I believe he was trying to find Jasmine."

"Really?"

"It was the same exact night that she disappeared."

Ari sighs and looks at her. "Oh, God. What a terrible…terrible thing."

"Yes. She had called him that very night, too."

"How do you know? Intuition?"

"Leon's cell phone charges come to me, Mr. Fisher. I recognized my granddaughter's number."

"Do you think you could trace her phone to find her?"

"Maybe I should hire somebody. But alas, I don't pay for Jasmine's calls. I wish I did, Mr. Fisher. I wish I did."

"I hope for her sake and yours that she turns up soon. Safe."

"If she even wants to be found. She is a troubled girl. I love her. But I can't help being angry with her about what happened to Leon. And I wish I knew who or what to blame for her behavior that night." Ari felt the room shifting in front of him. The dark walls nauseate him. "But perhaps there is no one to blame at all. How much easier that would be. My granddaughter is simply a willful, troubled creature as should have been apparent to anyone who knew her. In fact, I'm rather surprised you did not see it for yourself. Mr. Fisher, I must say, you don't look well right now. Are you alright?" Ari avoids her pitch tar eyes.

"I'm sorry, Mrs. Ng. I am," he takes his napkin and wiped his face. He thought he sounded just a bit too contrite. As if it were my own recklessness. "I mean, I didn't sleep very well last night."

Flashing him an alligator smile, Mrs. Ng suddenly moves closer in the booth towards him. "And why is that. Now tell me. Let's talk about you. Enough of my troubles. What's on your mind, Mr. Fisher?" Ari tried his best to concentrate. To his surprise he places his hand on her wrist and she folds her hot hand over his. Jasmine's grandmother; revived, ageless, ancient witch, vertiginous mistress, toxic concubine, gargoyle, coiled febrile monkey, rabid hissing bat, sorceress, high priestess, beating her leathery chest, curving in silhouette against the fire, swaying to the beating drums, blood of virgins flowing down her sweaty concave belly, receding from strident, throbbing ribs. Jasmine's ancient source. Tiny. Lethal. Mrs. Ng.

He recalls his choices for the day. Sleeplessness. The pointless, onanistic trek to Crescent City, to the foggiest tin can of all, the last place where anyone of record saw Jasmine. Mrs. Ng's goddamn granddaughter; Jasmine, slithered from the loins of a full blooded woman, the nameless mother, once herself a blue, slimy creature yielding from this here tiny beast, the fiery womb of this cawing creature with the soulless black eyes whose talon like fingers were now burning their way through his doughy, hirsute hand.

"Well that explains why you were asleep when I came into the lobby tonight. Yes?"

Ari attempted a smile. "Not the best way to make an impression, I'm sure."

She allowed a smile, even a wink before asking. "So why did you not get any sleep last night, my good Mr. Fisher?"

"I don't know, really. Every once in a while I have trouble sleeping."

"Troubles on your mind? Are you afflicted, Mr. Fisher?"

"Papers to grade," Ari reached.

"What else?"

"That's mainly it, just now."

"But that's just routine, isn't it? That's nothing at all to you. Tell me now. Don't be so superficial with me. That's not very interesting. Now what is troubling you?" Driving all night, recreating the last time I fucked your granddaughter, resenting my boss, dreading this very meeting with you Mrs Ng. "My ex is getting re-married. My son's moving away."

"Ah, information! At last. So you're divorced." Ari braces himself for questions about his marriage. "And you have children?"

"Just my son. He's joining the peace corps," he beamed. "So...he'll be gone for two years. I won't see my boy for quite a while." A smooth ball of rawness floated up his chest. Ari bit down, shocked by the imminence of emotion. Jesus. He swallowed it back down.

"You love your boy," she softly pronounces.

"Yes, ma'am," he stutters. He takes in his breath, grabs his linen, and tries to overcome his insurrecting grief with irritation at looking vulnerable. Dimly it occurs that this might in fact be useful to him. Suddenly, the emotion dries up.

"Well," she said. "I can see that. I'm happy for you. Not that he's leaving, but that you're proud of him. Yes? And so as a parent," she said, taking his arm. "I can trust that you understand me and my own situation a little bit better." Her touch is cool and dry and he catches a faint sepulchral odor of powder. He leans in a fraction of an inch it seemed, as if to better co-create their conspiratorial confessions.

"I've never had a child...."

"Die?" she whispers.

"No,"

"Go missing?"

"No. Neither."

"Of course not. I'm so glad, Mr. Fisher. Really. Now..." she slowly says, almost at a whisper, "let's say no more about it. Please."

"Yes, Mrs. Ng."

"I raised six children of my own."

"Wow."

"Hard to believe?"

"Not necessarily."

"I'm a little woman, of course," and she wraps her arm more fixedly around his own and fixes her black eyes upon him. "I've lived a full life. I brought my oldest children with me when I first came here. Alone, Mr. Fisher. One of them lived on. One of them did not. Flu! It was a long time before things got better. I worked and worked in a place where I was invisible to people like you."

"Like me?"

"Like us, I mean. Comfortable people is what I mean. Perhaps not untroubled, but comfortable. You know? Yes. People like us, yes, Mr. Fisher." She smiled, her incisors piercing through. "It was a long time before I became...one of us. So to speak."

"What happened?"

"What happened? I was a slave, Mr. Fisher."

"What?"

"Ha. Something like that. I was a piece worker. A seamstress. A faceless shop. No windows. Under the table. No, I never thought of myself as a slave, of course not. I was actually glad to feel relatively safe for my life. Eventually, I worked in a beauty shop and I went to school. And my daughter went to school as well. A very sad young girl, Jasmine's mother. You cannot blame her."

"Jasmine?"

"Yes, exactly. The better things got the more driven I became to make things better. Ten years after I arrived in this land, I owned and ran my first salon. Later I bought a second and my daughter ran it. You understand? She married, of course, the first chance she could, beneath her, mind you, to some kind of drifter, a sloe-eyed Mexican youth. So I got on with my life and by now I was able to attract and go toe to toe with a man of means and property. The man bought me two more stores, including a spa. And together we had four more children. Two of them died in child birth." Her voice remained steady, her eyes narrowed, her teeth threatened to burst from her crowded mouth.

"How terrible."

"My son, a captain in the U.S. marines; killed in a bomb blast in Iraq." Ari looked down at his hands, shaking his head in what he hoped

71

was a credible portrait of humility at another's absurdly large grief. Keep the platitudes to a minimum. Jasmine. He was humbled. Inadequate. Part of him doubted whether he had even heard her correctly. Or at all, as if he had only imagined that she had told him about her dead son. He spread out his fingers on the table looking at them. "Leon's father," she said, simply. "Ever since, I've practically raised him….So are you wondering?" he clearly hears her conspiratorial whisper. "Are you wondering how you must feel right about now, Mr. Fisher? Are you wondering how you might feel had you found out that something terrible, something unspeakable had just happened to your own son? To your Simon?"

Ari's head shoots up and he stares hard at her, glowing with a ready rage. His glasses had steamed, so he takes them off and calms himself while he cleans them yet again with an unused corner of his napkin. Before he can speak, Mrs. Ng resumes. "I can tell though. I know that even if you have never known what I've known, I know that you are real, Mr. Fisher. You love as I love. Don't you?" She was smiling and her tone seemed gentle again. For a moment something soft seemed to hover, to connect them, if only he wanted it to. Her smile falls suddenly and her face goes slack as she intones to him in a whisper, harsh like gravel. "It is a painful thing sometimes to love someone, Mr. Fisher. Yes?"

"Yes," he says. He considers that this might be true. "Yes, I suppose that sometimes it is."

"You suppose?"

"Yes."

"Well don't 'suppose'. Know! You do love your son?"

"Yes. Of course."

"And his mother. Did you love her?"

"I thought I did."

"You thought you did?"

"Yes."

"How vague an answer. Do you not know?"

"I've moved on. So has she."

"But was it not painful when the relationship ended?"

72

He pictured his beautiful, perfect wife in Paul Langford's sweaty embrace. "Yes, of course it was, Mrs. Ng. Divorce is very….dislocating."

"So is marriage, Mr. Fisher. It presents one with the opportunity to fully know oneself. But many instead only go deeper into their own confusion. Did you or did you not love her?" she asked him, trying to sound playful.

"With all due deference, perhaps we could change the subject just a little bit." Instead of withdrawing his arm, he found himself drawing closer, as if to be playful in return. How easy it would be to throttle her scrawny neck. He imagined himself doing so, the whole while whistling some saccharin tune, as if he were merely pouring cleaning fluid from a large container into a small container. One swollen sack emptying into another.

"But you see," she continues, "Either proposition is fundamentally tragic. You either loved her and saw that love die, or you never loved her at all and thus all you ever gained or lost was not in fact a relationship at all, but something else I have a different name for."

"Mrs. Ng…" he looks into her dark and savage face, traces the rivulets in her long, primitive brown neck, a knot of teakwood abutting her jagged clavicle. He takes in her talon like fingers and childlike, withered hands, and he calculates how easily all her bones might break in a lascivious embrace, crackling like desiccated tinder. "I'm not prepared to discuss…"

"What was her name?"

"Her name?"

"What was your wife's name?"

"Sabrina."

"Lovely name.

"Yes."

"Listen to me. We either have relationships or we have arrangements. They're not the same. Relationships with people, with life, the universe. Or we make arrangements. Not the same. Maybe what you had with Sabrina was merely an arrangement. In which case, all is now as it should be. The only thing that is tragic is longing for your own delusion. Now you needn't be embarrassed before me; both my husbands, my marriages, these were, at the end of the day, they were both arrangements. So I understand perfectly. And you know what? They worked. At least they worked based on the rules of these…arrangements." And she showed her teeth. "We had an understanding, a deal if you will. Very orderly, these arrangements. Relationships now. Not all orderly, not at all." She smiles and the lines on her weathered face seemed to flower and swim. "They're very…messy. Very messy." She takes a breath and continues, "And on occasion, these arrangements can get mistaken for relationships and vice versa. And when that happens. Well, that's another time that heartbreak occurs."

Ari notices his drink had been replenished. He reaches for it and takes a swallow. Momentarily refreshed, he looks at Mrs. Ng and rejoins, "Have you also had relationships, Mrs. Ng? Not just arrangements?"

"Oh yes. Most definitely. They weren't always happy or mutually agreed upon. But they existed."

"But not with your husbands?"

"With my grandchildren, Mr. Fisher."

Ari pays the check as Mrs. Ng coos about having a wonderful time. "I most definitely will inform Dr. Cameron and Dr. Abramson that you have a been a most gracious host and amiable dinner companion. You should feel very confident about that, Mr. Fisher." Ari smiles. But then he wonders. Perhaps she was mocking him. She knew he craves recognition and approval from a boss that he unaccountably dislikes. Had he not had too much too drink? "But of course, Mr. Fisher. The night is not quite over. Is it?"

They were headed towards the door. Ari realizes he has forgotten himself and is walking ahead of her. Abruptly he stops himself and starts to turn when he feels her bumping against him.

"Oh. Sorry."

"Not to worry," she insists, but she looks impatient to him. They step outside. Ari is immediately struck by the wasteland of fog that dominates and eclipses all, that seeks to seep inside of both of them, a gray and indeterminate dreamscape, intimate yet endless.

He stands for a moment thinking of what to do. She looks tired and suddenly much older to him. "I know you were looking forward to visiting Trinidad harbor. It's not far from here but we have to pass down a very steep, windy road. It might not be a good idea." She looks at him, her hat have covering her eyes. "Of course, I'll take you straight to your hotel so you can get some rest. This fog is very good for sleep, I find." The image of Leon Ng driving into the fog, into thin air, seems to hover in his words. Leon was looking for Jasmine. She had called him no doubt. Cousins, bound only by their losses. Ari looks at his watch. Eight forty-three was all. Yet it could still be another hour driving in this fog before he is back home again, this time to sleep, to sleep. And when he finally rises, he will drive to San Jose to engage in yet another errand that he dreads even more. He shakes the thought away and hopes that at least he might be rid of this Mrs. Ng within thirty to forty minutes, even if it meant suffering through awkwardly infuriating silence.

Casually, Ari speaks, "It's a shame you're all the way in Arcata. I myself live less than a mile from here." He blinks. What was the point of such a statement? But it was too late to take them back. She turns to look at him and though her eyes were unseen through the brim of her hat, he senses her eyes widening, a smile erupting.

"Well. How long do you imagine the fog will last?"

"Could be all night," he answers, the words clouding heavily in his throat.

"Well then. What do you think we should do?" She approaches him. "I'm a little bored at the thought of going home just yet. Besides, we are not yet finished yet. Are we? Maybe…maybe it is too foggy to driving long distances on poorly lit roads. I rely on your judgment in this matter."

Ari takes a breath, conscious of inhaling the fog itself. He stretches out the fingers of his hands, feeling them crack. "Well. Of course I'll be making sure you get back to the hotel, safe and sound."

"Of course. I would not expect you to leave me here, Mr. Fisher. What else?"

"Well. If you'd like to relax a little bit first with that night cap we had looked forward to - in the hopes the fog might lift a bit - I would be honored to be your host for a drink Chez Fisher."

"Chez Fisher?"

"Yes, Mrs. Ng."

"Ah. You live close by?"

"Maybe two miles at most."

"It's delightful. Purely delightful. Let us go to Chez Fisher at once."

"Very well then."

And she puts her arm in his elbow as though they were properly lady and gentleman and with that, he leads Mrs. Ng to his car, her powder tickling his nose, Ari fully aware that this was entirely an unwise plan, regardless of the outcome, thirty eight sleepless hours, drunk and overfed. He is like the driver and the engine of a car without gas, utterly self-sufficient, careening on a queerly exciting path, caring nothing for where he settles when the fuel finally runs out.

"Ah, what a lovely sanctuary this is," Mrs. Ng intones as if commenting on a stain she had found in the bedspread. She wanders briefly through the comfortable living room, hands locked behind her back, stopping at the window, staring out at the creeping gray of fog that conceals the manicured lawn of Ari's private grounds.

"Not much of a view, I'm afraid, Mrs. Ng. If it was clear, I could have turned on the lights and showed the trees and what an enchanted little spot I have."

She turns towards him, offering him a wry smile, pursed lips, almost a smirk. "Perhaps the fog itself will serve to enchant us. No?"

"You might say that."

"Yes, I might. In fact, I just did," she says taking one step towards him. "Do you like the fog, Mr. Fisher? Not just the trees and the rivers, but the very fog itself that nurtures them?"

"I suppose I do, actually," Ari admits. Guiltily.

"There you go supposing again. Well I in turn suppose that you like the fog a very great deal, actually. Would you agree?"

"Really? And how is that?"

"Right there for example. Answering a question with a question." She stands about three feet from him.

Ari is seated now in his plush and ample armchair. "You'll have to do better than that, Mrs. Ng?"

She lowers her gaze a bit and smiles. "I posed the question. Now you tell me."

"Well….I suppose. I mean, I would say that I like the idea…the effect rather, that I live in a magical world; you know, a place forgotten by time, protected by the mists and fogs, a place where nothing changes and where nothing can touch us."

She stands arms crossed, seeming to consider what he has just said. Then she walks away towards the window and looks out again as if trying to envision there the world he had just described. "That's candid, Mr. Fisher. Candid," she repeats still looking out, her back to him. "I get it. I feel it, too," she turns. "It's not the way of the world, you know. But right here, I feel it here in this place. With you."

The prospect of sleep recedes agonizingly away from him even as the fog rolls further in. Perverse possibilities in her unlikely presence keep him coldly alert. "Please Mrs. Ng. Do sit down?" She does so on the far end of the couch. "Can I get you anything? Coffee?" She asks only for water. The thought occurs that he could pour a shot of vodka into his own water glass. He does so and returns, hands her glass to her, and sits down, close to her.

"Mr. Fisher!"

"Mrs. Ng."

They make uncomfortable, heavy laden small talk for a few ambiguous moments. All evening, he had feverishly imagined either strangling or fucking her and of course it was impossible to do either. Yet he still entertained both scenarios, his restless mind detached from his weightless body. He wasn't right in his head, of that he was well aware. No, it was enough excitement, enough speeding through the fog to simply sit so boldly next to her, right beside her, drunk, sleepless, in his own den, wrapped in the sepulchral fog. It was maybe even more than enough to imagine Bud Cameron's reaction if he, the trusted servant, ruthlessly boned his money pot, his most powerful donor. Cameron's reaction. Sabrina's. Jasmine's. (My god, what has become of her?) Simon's reaction? His beautiful son. It was as if he forgot to breathe and in that struggle for breath, he felt himself about to fall, and unbidden, he jettisoned himself through the fog and off the road, soon to crash upon the rocks. Ari starts and finds himself choking on his drink. He coughs and spills some of his drink on the carpet. Curiously, Mrs Ng makes no perfunctory remarks of concern, he noted. He feels himself blanch and he asks himself, panic streaked, did I just black out again? He puts down his fire water, determined not to touch another drop of alcohol for the rest of the night (or for the rest of my life, perhaps, he ruefully considers).

"Are you alright then?" he hears her say at last. He nods and stands up to excuse himself for a moment. Instead of going to the bathroom, he wipes his brow with a paper towel in the kitchen and coughs. He would go with this thing, however ridiculous, just as long as there was any momentum. He would ride it, he knew. It was not a comforting thought, but it was a decision. "Mr. Fisher!" he hears her calling. He had begun to dislike the sound of his name on her lips. Perhaps she really was an alien, a silicon beast with sulfur for blood and acid in her pores. "I have been pondering again." Pondering? "About the allure of the fog for you. At this she draws up her legs so that she sits easily in the corner of his sofa, her bare feet like tarry hot coals.

"Do make yourself comfortable," he says returning to the couch.

She chuckles at the back of her throat, a dry, restless shushing. "Well. I believe in all earnestness that the fog for you represents… questions that don't need to be answered and answers that don't need to be sought."

"Riddle me this, you say," but his colon chills at what she's getting at. "Well, I thought that was what I already said. You know, the part about nothing changing and nothing touching us."

"Close. In a way. But it's more. It's solutions that need not be applied, memories that can be erased, fears and resentments absorbed. And absolved."

"My dear, what sharp teeth you have."

"Maybe absorbed. Or perhaps merely trapped. And yet it at least feels as this moment like everything has been muted, absorbed."

"It makes for a great night's sleep. I can tell you."

She leans forward. "Don't plan on sleeping much tonight, Mr. Fisher." And she puts her hand on his knee and his mind erupts and he is on the verge of reaching for her when she pushes off his knee to stand up. "Emptiness!" she declares.

"What?"

"Emptiness," she pronounces.

"Emptiness?"

"Emptiness… yes!" She suddenly seems intoxicated herself, breathing deeply through flared nostrils. "The fog, of course. Emptiness. And the fog, of course, quite naturally….is you, my friend," she concludes, pointing at him with a crouched hand, peering over it, winking at him.

"The emptiness is me," he rejoins, not offended. "I've heard that's where God is, Mrs. Ng. His voice is heard out of the emptiness."

"Lovely thought. But no, that is not at all the case we have here. The emptiness, and the fog in which it resides, is all about you. Nor do you believe or give a thought about God. Indeed, indeed."

"You seem very sure."

"Quite sure."

"You seem very proud of your conclusion."

"Not at all. Never confuse certainty for pride."

"What are you talking about?"

"Well, you can be certain and humble, just as you can be certain and proud. They are separate experiences. Although I am a proud person, it's true."

"No, no, I mean, what are you talking about that I am the emptiness. The emptiness. What is that supposed to mean, exactly?"

"What does that mean?" she says, very animated. "Just that. Emptiness."

"I don't understand, Mrs. Ng. That's why I asked. Enlighten me."

"Enlighten who?" she roars. Quieting herself. "There's no one in there, Mr. Fisher," she says, pointing. "Nothing."

"That's insulting."

She raises an eyebrow. "You are not insulted."

"No?"

"You are excited," she says taking a half step forward. "You are nothing. But appetite." She lowers he head and looks up darkly. "Appetite. Instinct. Dressed up, of course in charm, urbanity, well-dressed clothes and intellect. You're deliciously handsome of course. All the young woman, all the lost young girls. They must find you irresistible. Well-dressed, yes. But naked? Stripped of your urbanity?"

"Naked, yes," Ari responds. "Can you see me naked?"

She laughs dismissively. "Very funny, Mr. Fisher. Aren't we all, then? Naked?" And she shows her teeth. "Pure Id you are my friend."

"Aren't we all? Pure Id?"

"No! No we're not. You are. I'm not. Most people are not. Or if they are, they do not dress it up so well," and she takes another step towards him, slowly creeping until she stands within one urgent reach.

"I see," he feigns to go along, shutting out her curses, ready to have his way with a mute and wild animal. He swallowed the edge in his voice. "So I hide it well. My Id. Is it something for someone as sophisticated and insightful as you to see right through me. Is that it?"

"No, Mr. Fisher. That's not correct at all," and she cocks her head and gives him a narrow incredulous look. Her knee bumps up against his. She smiles her alien smile and turns away again. "You are only the fog it seems to yourself. To me and to anyone at all paying attention, you are as transparent as the waters that rush over the lifeless stones in the rivers."

Ari smiles. "That's a lovely turn of phrase --"

She cuts him off. "Let us recount, shall we. You were sleeping when I found you, most likely because you were up all night, carrying on

80

with what I shall not name. You arrived with several drinks to spare, again on no sleep. You ate like a bear. Most striking of all, there were several moments tonight when I felt you had actually left your own body and yet had not one tiny clue about it." Ari sits up, bolt awake, feeling his ears burning, his fingers tingling. "So you see, well dressed as you are. You are not so sophisticated. Maybe this is not you at all times. But it's no coincidence, I'm sure that you present yourself like so to me of all people." She floats slowly back towards him. "It's not so difficult to see, you know."

"I apologize," he weakly leaks.

"Don't even bother."

"It's true. I couldn't get to sleep last night."

Now she stands above him again, though just barely, for even as he sits back against the couch, she is just barely above eye level. "Something on your mind, Mr. Fisher?"

"Yes."

"Tell me."

"I prefer not." Jasmine.

"No?" she smiles again and cocks her head once more. "And to think that I actually expected more from you. Those young girls must be as lost or more so as you are."

"They aren't all so young," he offers recklessly.

"I might get it out of you yet. Whatever's really on your mind."

"I'm sorry I behaved at all badly and out of sorts."

"Because of no sleep?"

"Yes."

"And then you drink?"

"Normally I can handle it. I thought I was."

"Are you now worried, Mr. Fisher?"

"About what?"

"Two million dollars? A bad report to your beloved Mr. Cameron?"

"Dr. Cameron."

"Yes." Her smile broadens, teeth pushing against her cheeks again.

81

"Of course," he says, plainly, trying to smile himself.

She brushes her knee up against his own once again. He smiles. "Were you resentful at being sent off on his little errand? Holding hands with some musty, mothballed matriarch?"

"You're anything but that, I'll say."

"I'll take that as a 'yes'".

"Yes."

"Do you like Dr. Cameron?"

"What?"

"Do you like him? You heard me."

"He's alright."

"So you don't like him very much, I think."

"Not at all. I mean, that's not true."

"Really?"

"We generally stay out of each other's way."

"Really. Well. I stand utterly corrected," and she swings her braids again, rickety vipers. "Clearly you love and adore the man." Her little knee began undulating against his. Unmistakable.

"We generally leave each other alone. On a good day," and he smiles, chuckles, as does she, his dissembling falling away.

"Ah, Mr. Fisher, let me tell you exactly how much you love your dear *Doctor* Cameron?"

"Tell me. I eagerly await your pronouncement."

She looks at him level. "You love so much, that you'd like nothing more than to have your dirty little way with his school's greatest benefactor."

Ari laughs out loud. So now at last it's out in the open. And yet it makes him angry. "Mrs. Ng. I assure you that all this has nothing to do with Bud Cameron."

"You can assure me all you like. It has everything to do with Bud Cameron."

"And I assure you that the mention of his name is most definitely…a buzz kill," was all he could say, as stupid as it sounded in his ears.

"Your beloved Dr. Cameron?"

"Yes," now both of them began to laugh.

She was leaning in. "Are you high, Mr. Fisher?"

"Not on substance. But yes. I confess I am."

"On what then?" she whispered, gently parting his knees and floating in between them. "Power? Adrenalin? Doing everything you're not supposed to?"

"Of course," he confesses, breathlessly.

She pulls herself effortlessly to sit on his lap, facing him, yet holding herself straight, as if riding a horse, as if to delay just yet any further contact. "Let me ask you something, Mr. Fisher," she hisses.

"I want you to."

"I'm not so sure that you do. And I know exactly what you want. So…," she hovers near his ear. "What is it that scares you the most?"

"That's your question?"

"What are you most afraid of my dear? Are you so afraid to die?" And she began to rock slowly up and down. "There are so many ways for fools to die," she whispers, so softly, he cannot be sure he has heard her. His blood rushes everywhere inside of him. Once more she whips her braids, smack in his face this time, and she stares cat-like, slit eyed, coffin black. "Answer the question. Mr. Fisher." She rocks fiercely upon him, coiling and writhing, her dry, hot hands and nails scaling his ears and neck. "Answer the question. Answer it, for I have already answered it. Shall I tell you myself? I am not afraid. Death is very safe. Death is the least of all my concerns. But you…you Mr. Fisher. You are so very…so very afraid." She bears into him, black bottomless eyes, rocking herself, and his heart rises to his throat and his jaw falls slack and his hands bulge, ready to spring upon her to rip her clothes away and to split her in two, like a chicken wing devoured, sinew, cartilage, bone, and all.

What exactly happened next he was never to know.

Dimly, Ari senses turmoil. Tumbling. Everything is suddenly in free fall as though smashing through the fog, far beyond the flimsy guard rails, sailing unhinged, unplanned, before dashing upon whatever awaits below, impassive, hidden, and ruthlessly hard. He awakens at last, unsurprised to find himself thrusting mightily into Mrs Ng, a dark brown, smoldering branch, Shiva with teeth. His hands brace upon the bed, inches from her bony, dark, writhing shoulders. It was as if he had always been impaling her, wolverine roaring, overwhelming this tiny ferocious woman, teeth wailing. Hours, decades, eons seemed to pass. Until. In a blinding flash they clenched and he felt a kind of exhale hotly pass his throat, a white light, a taste of metal, his body charged, and she throws her head back, corded neck, silently screaming, throat proffered to him, eyes rolling away to some primitive aegis of her mind, stiffening against him, and he holds her still to empty out completely deep inside her lifeless womb, as if he could possibly have missed, but just to make his point. No accident. This is really happening. She is his. Completely.

She clenches further and then relaxes. Yet he is still not done with her. And so he continues beyond his point, wanting to talk dirty to her, but it wasn't sexy dirty, he knows. Instead, he wretches forth a cold, hard stream of curses that tears through him. He will never remember what incoherent thing he actually says, but he knows quite well how much he wants to shout out that of course he had fucked her precious granddaughter, many times, a crazy alley cat, that he was the last to have seen her, in a shroud of mist, that of course he had miserably disappointed the girl, for she fled from him, from that terrible motel room, and this was after he had first tracked her down to try and calm her, to talk some sense into her, to affectionately cajole her into coming back home, wherever that might be, maybe nowhere at all, only don't let it be here in this filthy, condom stinking hovel. It was of course because of him that Jasmine, alone, afraid, rejected, disappeared into the dark and dangerous street, quickly absorbed by the creeping, laughing, peripatetic fog, and he had had no business with her any way, but now he had made his pathetic attempt at rescue, but of course he only used her once again and her pathetic, idiot cousin Leon was also trying to protect her, trying

84

to find her - because of Ari, of course - trying to find his bleeding sister like a needle in the hungry fog, and like the ineffectual loser he was, Leon had driven off a cliff, had crashed into the molten sea, the hellacious rocks, and it's fucking true, he thinks, these Asians just can't fucking drive!

Ari grasps her hands like they were roped to the bed, feels her tiny fingers, squeezes and wanting to crush her little bones in his final furious rage. He feels himself melting and before that happens he wants so badly to curse her again, to call her disgusting, bigoted names, sweat streaming from his forehead. At last he is still. In the sudden silence he feels suddenly that he is alone. Something, something was terribly, terribly wrong.

Something was terribly wrong. Mrs. Ng lies unnaturally still, her eyes lost in the back of her head. He stares at their egg white emptiness. He stands naked, wet, glistening, wanting to feel triumphant, lordly, amped on adrenalin, a grim, chaotic, candy glazed high, sleepless, drunk, improbably enraged. Are you glad you asked me now, ol' Bud? Two million dollars literally fucked up. Dizzy. Inside himself, knowing, not wanting to know that something was horribly wrong.

He stands naked, hairy, muscular, yet lumpy, dangling, unkempt, meaty, lewd. The adrenalin begins to fade. He looks at Mrs Ng. whose head is still thrown back, her throat exposed. He knows. He won't say the words to himself, but he knows. Makes himself look at her face directly, and just at that moment her eyes roll back to meet him squarely staring at him. Through him. He heart clenches and he staggers back, nearly toppling. "Mrs Ng! Mrs. Ng!" he shouts, fearfully, hopefully. "Are you OK?" he blurts, stepping further away from her. He closes his eyes, tells himself to relax to breathe. He dares to touch her hand, limp, cool, and heavy. Ari recoils.

In that monstrous voice of her, he imagines her saying, 'Of course I'm OK, Mr. Fisher. My troubles are over. Forever. You, on the other hand, Mr. Fisher.." No, they never did cross over to address each other on a familiar first name basis, he thinks. They remained strangers to each other until the end.

What's left of her naked body is already a discarded shell. For the first time it seems he is actually seeing her. Clearly, she had been delicately beautiful, at least at one time. But now indeed she appears to him plainly as an old woman, her skin loose fitting and dry. Her midsection is beset with scars, outrages no doubt from multiple C-section births. Yet there were other mysterious defects and wounds along her upper body and throat, all of which were - to his relief - ancient looking, hoary fossils, testaments to unnamed traumas.

What happened?

'Mr Fisher, you need not know. I have seen and fought and evaded many things that you could have no idea about,' he imagined her saying. But she was gone now; she had escaped and rudely left her tired, insinuating, inconvenient body behind for him to dispose of. A corpse in his own bed. And so he thinks, what am I going to do? Ari casts about to see the time. Ten-forty six. It was earlier than he thought, yet it was still very late, indeed. What am I going to do? It occurs to him that the decisions he makes in the next few minutes could potentially be the most important of his entire life. He tries to still his addled mind. Take a shower? Alright then. He takes his shower, hot water, corpse in his bed, chasing away momentarily the fatigue and the very top thin rime of shame weakly clinging to him.

Mrs. Ng's curse. No sleep for him tonight.

He dresses in jeans and a sweatshirt. Of course the body had not moved. Rubs his face, tries to think of what's his next move. (Bury her) The right thing to do was to call the police and pretty damned quick. Right? Now what would be the result of that? (Bury her). That would set in motion a hellacious shit storm, likely resulting in his disgracing the school, losing his job, his entire life style, and even implicating him criminally to the police. Had he not been drinking? He would no doubt be detained at least long enough to miss his son's party tomorrow night. No? Ari didn't know. Call the police right now and you'll probably stay out of jail. (Bury her.) Time elapses. Precious time. Ten-fifty five. Wouldn't the coroner, or some such person, be able to determine the time of death? Clearly, he did not murder her. Right? The complexities of their arrangements nauseated him, but they were completely private, compartmentalized. (You killed my grandson, destroyed my granddaughter, you callow, arrogant, prick. After you bury me, I will bury you with your precious tinny, empty career. You'll have nothing left because all you are is an inflated ego with nothing but empty lust crouching in the dark until you can take others down with you. Now I am safe and sound. Go ahead and bury me. Then I shall bury you. Bury you. Alive. My good, Mr. Fisher.)

He had never seen a dead body before. It was one of the quietest objects he had ever seen. To his relief, he felt no further possibility that this corpse would suddenly come to zombie life, its head rotating 360, its nakedness still glistening, raw with exertions and obscene leaking of their coital ruckus. At this last observation, something quickly fell then rose inside him, and he raced back into the bathroom to purge himself of the acid rancid remnants of undigested flesh.

Like it never happened. (Bury her!) I'm not even a human being. Mrs. Ng was barely the size of a young child, a withered husk, dark and tinder like, ready to be discarded beneath the ground.

'Ari Fisher," he listens to the voice of Bud Cameron. Clenched teeth. 'I blame myself. I really do. I gave you a chance to be trustworthy and you fucked not only Mrs. Ng, you fucked me, you fucked this school, and you fucked your entire future. Are you satisfied? What in God's name is wrong with you? You self-involved, arrogant, narcissistic bag of rotting shit. You preening, strutting, pompous asshole; you useless, disgusting, pile of vomit.'

His erstwhile anger and resentment towards Cameron turned toward inward, an appalling throb of scalding fear, regret, and loathing. What the hell had you against Bud Cameron, anyway? Had he really hated working for the man that much? Time was elapsing. He stands indecisive, melting. One call and he could still end all debate. Goddamnit, though, he wasn't ready yet to throw away his life as he still thought he knew it. There had to be a way to make this all go away, to lose it all into the fog.

What had he done? Had intercourse with a consenting woman who despite her chronic heart disease had made her choices, lived and died the way she chose. (Did you black out?) Of course, he had no memory of several terrible minutes. She sat on my goddamn lap and grinded her little monkey body insanely against mine! Only the obvious could have happened. Eleven forty three already. (Bury her!)

He goes to his desk in the study, opens the drawers, rummages through his papers and at last finds what he wants. Expiration date, December 2014. Passport. Voice after voice piles in on him. You'll lose everything anyway if you run. Run where? You'll never come back. Your life is over anyway, lost in limbo. Can you even access your money? Will they freeze your accounts? (They?) You'll put yourself under suspicion of murder, you moron. (Not if they never ever find a body.) What's the alternative? Go about your business as if nothing has happened? (Maybe). They'll be looking for her and then they'll be looking for you. (Bury her!) Call the police. Right now! Every minute you wait, the more suspicion begins to fall upon you. His heart races. Do I even have a heart? Am I still even remotely a human being? A homo sapien?

The thought of Sabrina fall lightly all around him. He shakes it. A strange deflation squeezes him, sucking the air and the energy from himself. Ari just wants to lie down, to curl up, to disappear. Just lie here. Sleep. Sleep and then to wake up….in some other place, some other time. Wake up into a dream, bright, coiling fog. How about upon the trail? The soft, fecund trail, where he had fallen. Yes, even that. Of course. He would be grateful to settle for that. What if he had fallen asleep in the mists and this was the dream, right here? Now would be the time to awaken. Only eleven in the morning. His least favorite moment of the day; that it might reclaim him now, give him a kiss, the chance to hobble back and to sleep a blameless sleep, ocean or no ocean.

Or what if I reawakened and perhaps I'm back in San Jose. Sabrina is lying on her side. Simon sleeps down the hallway, or maybe he is even up, playing on his computer; I could talk to my little buddy, ask him what's keeping him awake, ask him if he's had a bad dream. Ari is there to protect them both, mother and son, but sometimes it feels like it might be the other way around. He and Sabrina don't talk but everything is still fine, still pleasant and comfortable and safe and their jobs and their routines and their friends do not threaten, no pestilent rotting exhales from their memories. Dinner parties. Sabrina might have had had a drink or two of Chardonnay. Ari drank vodka. But it was OK to loosen up and to entertain and to get loud and make everything bright and funny and witty and sparkly, and occasionally he and Sabrina would make intense love afterwards and at times he failed to remember it much. When they fought and Simon was little, the boy would begin to cry in his room. First Sabrina, then Ari would go into comfort him, to assure him that all was fine. And Ari took his satisfaction that he was always the last to say goodnight to him. They did not go in together.

"Hey buddy, do you want a story?" The boy was barely five. Perfect cheek.

"I don't know."

"You don't know? You always like a story," Ari affirmed, smiling.

"Maybe," Simon said. Sadly. It annoyed Ari. Because it saddened him. Even after three vodkas.

"Hey kiddo. Let's revisit the gentle sorcerer and his nemesis, the beautiful, but deadly black with from the land of Nog."

"His what?"

"Hmmm?"

"Dad. What's a nemo....You use dumb words."

"Nemo....Nemesis? Sorry, son. It means the witch is kind of like his enemy. But also his friend. Their friendship causes their enmity. And their enmity causes their friendship."

"That's a dumb story. I don't like it."

"Oh," Ari was a little abashed by this. "I'm sorry. You used to like it."

"I like Nog, though. There's nice things and stuff in Nog."

Ari smiled and kissed Simon on the cheek. Beautiful boy. Clever, too. Too smart for me. Sees right through me. "How about if I just tell you about things and stuff in Nog? Forget about sorcerers and witches." Simon just shrugged, his lower lip poofed out. "Or maybe you could tell me some things or ask me some questions." No response. Except for a slight frown that suggested his son was either mystified or bored, or both. "I'm sorry, buddy. I love you, kiddo. Maybe you're just really tired."

"No, I'm not," the boy insisted, just before being overtaken by a yawn.

"See that now! See. The land of Nog is calling you," and he playfully grabbed his little boy as if to scrunch and tickle him and the boy giggled but then got thoughtful. "I don't want to go to Nog, daddy."

"To sleep then. The land of sleep. How about that?"

"I don't want to dream, though."

Ari's face grew soft. "Do you have any dreams you don't like?"

"Yes."

"Are there any special ones?"

"Yes. They're scary. "

"Tell me, kiddo. They can't hurt you, you know."

"But they're scary."

"I know. Tell me about them."

"Dad?"

"Yeah, son."

"Are you mad at mommy?"

"What? No. Of course not. No. Why?"

"Because. You two never come in together."

"Come in together?"

"In here, Dad!"

"Oh....well, I know. That's so each of us can have some special time with just you alone." That seemed to satisfy the boy a little bit. He shrugged. But then he became thoughtful again.

"Daddy?"

"Yeah, baby."

"Why is there a dead, naked lady on your bed?"

Ari gasps for breath and stumbles against his desk, braces himself, and in the darkness of his upturned eyes, he slips down on his knees, groping at the air, clinging to something dry and safe in his right palm. His passport.

90

He emerges into action mode. Two glasses of water from the tap, gulped down urgently. Determined to make this problem disappear. His first impulse, which he quickly dismissed as madness was to simply grab the shovel from the garage and to commence digging somewhere beyond his property, perhaps near the trail where he fell that morning. But the folly of this was soon evident and he felt himself returning to his senses. The last thing he needed was Mrs. Ng's corpse reemerging in the next and certain deluge, glistening from the downpour, exhaling steam as the mists coiled upwards out of the metallic rain.

To his surprise, it was nearly midnight. Soon, a brand new day to eclipse the sleepless turn of the earth. No turning back. Time to remain in his right mind. Right here and now. Too much precious time was already lost. A plan had formed.

He strips the bed with the corpse inside, sedulously avoids direct contact with the leathery, rotting statuette. Ari ties the sheets together. Then he thinks and strides to his kitchen searching for his flashlight in the bottom drawer and from there casts out into the darkened garage, the light from his torch creating a weak and penumbral haze, until he can find the switch. Stalking inside the stillness of the garage, he finds at last the dusty, mulchy box he was looking for, his stash of hefty bags for tree trimmings in which he manages just barely to stuff the entire mess of sheets and watery bones and dry, flaccid flesh. This he will take somewhere where it can never be found.

But before disposing of the body, he realizes he must create for himself some cover, something that erases the trail to himself. (And I had better get rid of these goddamned sheets as well!) He makes his way back to the living room and finds Mrs. Ng's purse. And her clothes! Every trace of her he would have to be rid of. Something hard and blade like squeezes hot in his gut and he hates himself and his whole world fades to crumpled, bleeding orange. For a moment. Ari steels himself to enter his hand inside the purse, rummaging blindly through soiled crumpled tissues, powder cake dust settled throughout. Mrs Ng had been a secret slob. He finds her hotel key, still held within the paper sleeve provided. Room 219. It feels to him as if he were violating her very flesh yet again, the flesh once eagerly soiled, rotting rapidly now, and his heart races and his stomach protests and he clenches down against the phantom smell of his own bile moaning and lolling to seethe outward.

Slowly, Ari backs his car out, finds the path back to the road and steadies himself for the first leg of his long task. The fog is now miserable, unwelcome and nearly impenetrable, but he is accustomed to navigating where perhaps others could not. Slow going. More than once thought he feels the icy grip of Leon Ng's inevitable panic at outdriving the road and long into oblivion.

It annoyed him greatly that he was headed in exactly the opposite direction from where he really needed and intended to go. But instead, he stuck to the plan, heading to the very last place he wanted to go. Back to Mrs. Ng's hotel.

Ari kept a small bottle of vodka compartment to steady himself and to keep him company for the night. But he would not drink it. Not just yet. He could not risk yet another black out, this time driving in the fog with a corpse in his trunk. The plan was simply to make it look like she had first returned to her hotel and had in fact slept in her own bed that night. While inside her purse, his fingers had slid across many cards and identifications before finding her room key card, magnetized with the image of Arcata's uncharacteristically blue sky surrounding the hotel. Now Ari crept along the road, recognizing the straight away as his cue that he was almost there.

The fog was neither soothing, nor peaceful.

It matched his surreal grip on the next present moment. And so what am I doing? The only thing I can do to save my life as I know it and to spare my son from ever knowing. Now I'm committed. No turning back, even if I wanted to. And I don't want to. So the rest should be easy. He'd drive to the hotel, enter the room, muss up the bed, fluff some pillows, make it look like she had slept there all night. (But wouldn't it be obvious to any detective that the sheets were too clean to have been slept in? Might they at least be slower to notice anything amiss? He did not know. He could not care. He decided his plan was the most measured, the most rational, the one that bought him the most time.) He gripped the steering wheel at the base of his fingers as if he could throttle himself for being so astoundingly base and stupid and reckless.

Perfect! It had all been perfect and he had pissed it away. Do over. Rewind. But now this was the best he could to do to erase and rewind that which was indelible and irreversible. He had pocketed the key, pocketed his passport. While in his bedroom, the death chamber, he clenched and grunted at the waxy, deflated corpse, wrenched the sheets, fitted and flat alike, threw it over what had been her face and with a bark of rage over the rest of the discarded body, tightening it all into an awkward mound, nearly retching at the feel of the bony projections.

He rolls down the windows to help him stay awake and alert and here. Turns up the radio, try to find something loud and rhythmic. Scattered taillights and street lamps appeared. He realizes he has passed the airport and so he exits and makes his way back along the frontage road. There it was, only a few moments away, the airport driveway, multi storied lights perennially shining, chasing swirls of persistent fog. A tower peeks darkly out, the hotel, a shadow encased in a halogen glowing shroud of vapor. Slowly he circles the building, amazed at the distant sort of way that he presently feels nothing at all. He creeps along the parking lot, rolling like a snake's head to the back entrance. The lot is nearly empty and he pulls into the spot nearest the door, even though he's sure it's painted as a handicapped spot. Involuntarily, Ari flashes on what he might tell the manager on duty if he's spotted. Yes, your guest, and mine, I suppose, Mrs. Victoria Ng, she got some sort of food poisoning or something; so I stripped off her clothing and wrapped her tightly in sperm soaked sheets and stuffed her in this garbage bag and now I thought I'd drop her off and let you all share in the responsibility. It was a very stupid plan, of course, but he decides it is the best that he can do. Here he is. Right here. Right now.

Ari feels for the key in his jacket. He grabs his car keys as well and buoyed by anger, he jumps out of his car, imprudently letting the door slam, continues walking towards the hotel back door, a glass door, inserts the key. Green light. The lock snaps free and he opens the door, enters the back hallway which is surprisingly warm and clammy. There is the lively hum of the vending machine. Ari turns and makes his way towards the door leading to the stairs.

A new thought pierces his head. Visions of police at his home within twenty minutes of his first realization that she might be dead. You did the right thing by calling us. In his mind's eye he stands in his bedroom with the policemen and the corpse, standing butt naked, unwashed and glistening. He stands like this so as not to change anything about the scene, to keep things in order, to preserve integrity, to facilitate the investigation, naked, unclean, unwashed, available, raw and truthful, ready for the inspectors and the inspection. The police, the mortuary representative, the bulky youths in gloves come to intern the remains, the plain unapologetic truth. They nod and take furious notes as he stands there naked telling them everything. They appreciate his candor.

But this is not so with Bud. Not Bud. You what? What? All you had to do was have dinner. Take her to dinner. Be charming. Don't fuck her. Don't fuck her to death you selfish prick. Don't kill her. Don't disgrace yourself and all of us. Is that too fucking much to ask, that you simply not kill our donors? And I am not even a human being, he tells himself. And it's almost soothing, calming to him. I'm not even a human being, who would act like this, literally holding the bag, not the truth, and he walks down the dead and still, brightly lit sterile hallway.

He stands before Room 219. The green light flickers at the whisk of the key and he opens the door. A powdery warm odor greets him and he flinches, a living odor. Ari reaches around for the light but there isn't one on the wall. A weak shaft of light from the window creates the room in outline. He reaches for the bedside lamp and finds the switch. The bed is already unmade. Had she taken a nap? Perhaps his entire trip was pointless. Cautiously, he steps further inside. Ari peers inside the bathroom. There were tiny crystal bottles of ointments and perfumes, ghostly illusions of a lingering, undisturbed existence. Back in the bedroom, he finds her leather suitcase, half open, undergarments peeping out.

It hits him that he must dispose of all of it, every bit. It has to look as if she packed and left the hotel. There was no doubt she was expected to check out tomorrow regardless and return to San Francisco. Her room of course was paid for already. Twelve-forty seven. Ari commenced to work furiously to quietly pack her belongings. He rifles through the drawers and nightstands, in the bathroom, and stoops to the carpet for a pair of tiny stockings or lacy underwear. Mrs. Ng was a bit of slob, it turns out, in her room as well as in her purse.

He feels sickened, his head squeezes in a dry, rageful headache. A dark press of futility steals again through his actions. Soon he will be on the road again, he thinks, that somehow the worst will be over, despite knowing full well that the most dangerous part of all lies ahead. He would have to drive perhaps hundreds of miles with overwhelmingly indicting evidence of murder bursting from his trunk.

Ari notices his own rank odor of sweat and alcohol, even worse. No doubt he had left large bucketfuls of screaming DNA upon every handle, everything he touched. He grabs a hand towel, smears it with hand soap, and begins smearing it over countertops, lamp switches, faucets, preparing to wipe the inside and outside door handles before he leaves. He looks at the suitcase again and groans. How much riskier it would be for him to carry that thing out the door should anyone see him.

A sound catches his breath. A slip of paper pushes below the door. A note from the dead woman's ghost? From the police? Bud Cameron? His son, come to team up with him and to rescue him? Sabrina misses him and wants him back? But of course it was only the check-out receipt. And a kind of warning. Ari remains still to remain where he stands for several more minutes while the clerk continues to innocently haunt the hallway.

Ari paces the room, continuing to sweat profusely, yet feeling chilled and achy. The sweat seems to seep through his shoes and to soak inside the carpet as if shouting his name. He wanders into the bathroom in search of another unused hand towel. One left on the shiny metal bar.

Ari tears his glasses off and wipes his face and hands and he throws the towel down on the bone white floor. No, asshole. Pick it up. Take that as well and he bends over and the floor begins to pulse, expand, contort. Shit. I'm gonna pass out on this floor. Maybe I should just take off all my clothes right now, crawl into bed, and get some desperate sleep before first housekeeping, then the manager, then the police, and finally, Bud Cameron all arrive. He'll grin, smile, and wink. 'Surprise!" he'll shout. Someone thinks that's funny, slaps him on the back and curdles his gut in its claw, rolls his head and his gut and Ari falls to his knees and heaves into the perfect toilet a coral brown viscous string of bile, followed by explosions of undigested beasts and sea creatures. With relief he has rid himself of his lewd, excessive consumption. Finally, he rises, wiping his mouth with the back of his hand, while the room dims and flushes with golden pulses and yet again he realizes he is on the verge of passing out or blindness, until finally the screen dissolves and Ari manages to lean against the wall, breathing shallowly.

After a long silence, staring out the peephole, checking his pockets and having checked and wiped the room one last time, Ari is finally ready to leave. He opens the door, pulling the suitcase behind him. The corridor is empty except for enclaves of doors on either side, receding to the end. He walks, aware of how hard his breathing sounds to him. He finds the stairwell, grabs the metal rail and makes his way down, and as he turns the corner, his shin smacks the railing hard, meat pounded over bone, and overlaying a cut from the previous morning on his jog and before he can stop a short cry punches its way out from him and he drops the suitcase and grabs his shin. And he clenches down and feels every nerve in his neck tightening, sweat poring, and he takes a shallow, impatient breath.

He straightens himself and opens the door and a young man stands at the other end shooting receipts beneath doorways. How could he still be here? The man looks to be about twenty-two, wearing an ear piece connected to his phone. Ari freezes, infuriated. The man looks up and smiles at him. Ari smiles as well. The man nods and seems to smirk resuming his task.

Dead. Dead! I'm dead. Fucked! It's over. Over! Ari wipes his brow, gives what he imagines is a charming grin and a thumbs up sign. Yes, a thumbs up sign will make him both forgettable and legitimate. Checking out early at one in the morning instead of nine.

That's how it goes. Ari imagines how ghastly he must look. Perhaps it's hard to notice even at this modest distance. Hopefully.

The kid has not even seen his absurd gesture and resumes his task, turning back to exit on the opposite end of the hallway. Why the fuck was he still even here? He doesn't give a shit, though, and Ari bangs the suitcase into the door and struggles his way out. Does this kid even know his guests by sight? He works in the middle of the night. Does he recognize luggage? Really? Did you see anything at all unusual last night? Yes, the detectives will ask this goofy kid for anything that might help locate the whereabouts of some missing elderly dowager. Well yeah, there was this one guy I'd never seen before carrying a heavy suitcase, leaving the building at about one in the morning. Does that count as unusual? I mean, people come and go all the time around here. Well...maybe son. Maybe. In fact, it is precisely unusual, tell the truth. Tell me, was this man sweating at all? Did he give you a fucking thumbs up sign in some lame ass attempt to look normal to you? The boys eyes will widen as he exclaims, Goddamnit, he did, officer, he certainly did.

Ari opens the trunk, praying that neither the young man would come out, nor a phalanx of well-dressed and armed security officers, nor that Mrs. Ng's dead and skeletal arm should fly out at him, clutching his throat in its grip. Yes, I am praying, but to what. What kind of God will listen to such prayers? He stares at his filthy cargo. It was just a lumpy, heavy duty garden trash bag, stuffed in the trunk, fitting deftly atop a layer of old magazines and journals. The dead lumpy trash bag fits snugly on top. Lots of trunk space in his Lexus. But the suitcase doesn't fit, so he closes the trunk and puts the suitcase on the floor of the back seat. As a nod to caution, he places his jacket on top of it.

It is one fourteen now in the ante meridian post-midnight velvet dream time. The fog must surely still be choking the freeways. Ari's enormous relief at leaving the hotel quickly spirals downwards. He is done with this, though precious little it may have done him. And now, he knows for certain he will complete this mad errand. And then finally to sleep. His eyes bulge dryly from his forehead, stinging.

Ari grips the steering wheel, the windows rolled down, hoping to jump start his flagging spirits and energy. Desperate for coffee, he winds his way back to Trinidad to the all night station, fills his tank, buys a large coffee with syrupy cream. Again, he braves the sweats, risking the scrutiny of the bored clerk. He wipes his forehead with some napkins before making his purchases, including three chocolate bars with nuts. Finally his chest begins to loosen as he hits the 101 north once more. Moments later he begins his descent into that narrow strip of land separating ocean from lagoon, his aqua vista exploding into view as the fog is thinner here. He is admiring still this mystical point when suddenly his rear view mirror is flooded with an hysterical cluster of flashing, colored lights, piercing his car. Yes, it's a cop, a goddamn cop! (Fucked! Over!)

Ari slows the car and pulls over in the dark to the wide dirt shoulder. (Fucked!) In the fulcrum of his gathering despair, a remote balm of relief dwells in the deep. Maybe it's better if this is all over and done. Maybe he should just let go and slide down the snow and over the cliff.

He cuts the engine, the cop rolling in behind him, bloody corpuscles of light furiously circulating while the squad car's brights also flood Ari's car from behind. In the few seconds he knows he has before the officer arrives, Ari searches below the passenger seat where he remembers to look for a box of facial tissues. He blows his nose, wipes his forehead, still beaming with sweat, takes a swallow from his sugared coffee, scorching his tongue. Ari barely hangs on, his fingers trembling, splotched with little drops of coffee, he manages to return the cup to its holder near the seat. He grips the steering wheel and listens to the sound of his own breathing. There's a moment of silence broken by the crackling of the radio. A long, long time seems to pass while the cop takes his goddamn time. Ari fills the void, envisioning himself popping the trunk and hurling the bag of corpse and semen stained sheets upon the ground at the policeman's feet, whirling himself around and laying himself down against the hood, hands folded behind his back, screaming, Hurry, Hurry, the entire time.

At last the driver door of the squad car opens and a tall, athletic looking officer, boots and helmet, bearing a scimitar like torch, strides towards him while Ari gazes at his reflection in the side mirror, shrinking at his approach. Standing now at Ari's passenger window, the cop trains his flashlight on him, forcing Ari to squint, shrinking further, desiring to defecate. The cop raps upon the window.

Ari lowers the window, the salt of the ocean recalling its nearness and beckoning him to its endlessness, to its oblivion. "Good evening, officer," he says, the words sputtering out softly. Still, he continues to grip the steering wheel.

"Driver's license and registration," comes the curt but youthful sounding reply.

"Certainly. Certainly," Ari replies in a high pitch tone, rudely aware that he is once again sweating and likely emitting the sour stench of alcohol. Grimly he reaches towards the glove compartment. "My registration is in here," he announces, as he opens it, rummaging through maps and receipts in the obscene light from the car and the flashlight. Finally, Ari finds it. "Here you go," Ari offers hopefully, as if he were a poor student making his meager but sincere offerings to an indifferent professor.

The officer wordlessly receives Ari's license and papers and briefly inspects them. "This registration's expired," he announces.

"Oh. Sorry. I'm so sorry. I paid up just recently. It might be sitting on my desk at home, just arrived."

"Alright. Please state your address for me." Ari does so. "Wait here. Keep the engine off. I'll be right back."

Ari nods and sinks back into his seat, imagining himself confessing everything, ready to surrender, to say a thousand times that he was sorry. Sorry. Sorry. He recalls one of the many times when he had apologized to Sabrina for a hurtful remark or a neglectful attitude. 'I'm sorry.' Towards the end, he finally admitted that these words came easily to him, for they weighed so little, his catechism of regret, his theatre of contrition. She thanked him for finally telling the truth. Often when they were first married, she began to surprise him by saying, 'Why are you sorry?' And at first he'd take this to mean that she never thought he had wronged or slighted her at all. But he soon learned otherwise. She was looking to see what lay beneath the catechism. If anything. He could see her putting on her make up. Make up. The preparing of one's face. Studying her face in the mirror, she queried, 'Sorry for something you've done or said, or didn't do or say, or are you just sorry because you don't want me to be upset and you want everything to be nice and you can go back to sleep.'

'I'm sorry you're such a bitch, Sabrina,' is what he thought. 'Screw you.' He had in fact said nothing of the kind. But she ceases her make-up and she looks up at him through the mirror as if he had really spoken.

Ari is still gripping the wheel more fiercely than ever when the officer finally returns and hands him back his documents. "There you go, Mr. Fisher."

"Thanks."

"I pulled you over because your left tail light is out. I should be able to see both your lights, even in this fog. Also, you were drifting a bit across the lane divider while coming down the hill just now."

"Oh…I'm sorry."

"That can happen in this fog. But all the more reason why you have to be careful out here. You're on a dangerous stretch of road."

"Yes, officer."

"We're famous for our tsunamis. I haven't seen one yet. But we get accidents almost every night when the fog acts up like this."

"That's the truth."

"I need to ask what you're doing driving out here so late at night."

Ari looks up. "Is that a problem, officer?"

"Mr. Fisher, you can drive out on this public highway anytime you are competent to operate your vehicle safely. But since you're driving slightly erratically, I need to ask you what you're doing. For your own safety and the safety of other drivers. Answer the question, please."

"Of course. Well," he sighed. "I was working at home…I was grading papers and I got restless and decided to come out to the beach, you know, to get some air, a second wind. Sometimes I do that."

The cop writes something down on his pad. Without glancing up, he asks, "Grading papers."

"Yes. At Redwood, yes. I'm an instructor. It's the end of the semester, so I'm hustling to get done grading as quickly as possible. Let all my students know how they did, too."

"Alright, Mr. Fisher. Just as long as you're not 'hustling' down this highway in the fog. Understand?"

"Absolutely, officer."

"Mr. Fisher, have you had anything to drink this evening?"

"Yes," Ari asserts, feeling his confidence returning a bit. "I was out to dinner with one of our school donors and I had a couple of drinks with her at dinner, around eight o'clock or so. Nothing since."

"I see. And how many drinks do you recall having?" The officer's tone sounded more curious than interrogatory.

"Oh. Two at dinner time." Ari reflects. "You know, I did have a third one, I mean a first one before dinner," he adds, feeling shrewd. No one believes the two drinks story.

"Two drinks?"

"Three."

"I want to have you please step out of the car."

"I'm sorry?"

"Step out of the vehicle for me please, Mr. Fisher." The radio crackles and hisses. Ari's eye level is at the officer's gun riding heavily on his belt. He wonders about getting out, having mastered gripping the steering wheel.

"OK...sure." Ari opens the door and starts to turn when the seat belt stiffens and yanks him back. "Sorry," Ari blurts, restraining a curse, feeling his eyes tear up.

"What's that?"

"Nothing, officer," and he releases the belt, opens the door, plants both feet on the dirt, and steps up, his entire lower body matted in sweat, his underwear cleaving to his anus. Ari stands straight, holding onto the door with his right hand. Suddenly Ari is semi blinded by the beam of the cop's flashlight trained directly into his eyes. Instinctively, Ari flinches and holds his left hand in front of him. Again, he suppresses

101

the longing to defecate. Might they give him at least a little dark cell with a blanket where he could sleep a little?

"Follow my finger," says the cop, and at first, Ari cannot even find it through the wash of light, but there it is now, and the cop slowly moves his left forefinger back and forth. Ari smiles, easily able to follow it. "Please walk five steps towards me, putting your right foot directly in front of your left foot, and so on." The cop backs up to wait for Ari. "Now, Mr. Fisher."

Ari does so, looking at his feet, the coffee carving out focus in his head. No way could I grade a goddamned paper right now, but I can put one foot in front of the other. Calm. Slow. The flashlight beam drops. "You can stop now. Alright, Mr. Fisher, I regret I had to ask you to do this, but it's for your safety and the safety of others."

"Of course, officer."

"You don't seem drunk. But you do look like you could use some sleep."

I don't seem drunk? A fucking miracle. "I think you're right about needing to sleep."

"Did you know that driving with too little sleep is just as dangerous as driving drunk?"

"It is?"

"Yes, indeed. It's not exactly illegal, but I'm here to protect you and others on the road."

"Yes, of course."

"You live in Trinidad?"

"Yes. How did you know?"

"Your license. Remember?"

Ari attempts a wry smile. "Yes, of course. My license."

"I need to ask you to drive no further out tonight, but to make sure you drive directly and safely home."

"Certainly."

"I'm just gonna write a fix-it ticket for the tail light. There's no penalty or fine you know. Just get it fixed within seven days."

"Fair enough, officer." The cop proceeded to write again, using the high beams of his car for light. "I wanted to ask you," Ari says.

102

"Maybe I should rest a little before going home. The whole point of my drive was to come to this very point. Across the street. To breathe in the ocean. Would that be alright? Just to relax a few minutes over there, in the parking area, of course. Then home. Would that be pushing my luck?" Ari's eyes fall on the cop's name badge above his shirt. Cameron!

"I'll let you pull over there a little bit, Mr. Fisher. It's open, even though we don't like people hanging out there late at night. But you be careful. I want you home in bed as soon as possible."

"That's absolutely what I want as well."

"Are you able to drive home safely tonight, Mr. Fisher? You need to be straight with me."

Ari peers at the young man's face as if for the first time. Callow blond, barely out of adolescence, small, anxious features. "Yes. Officer Cameron."

"Because I can follow you home or part of the way."

"I'm fine. It's true I'm a little tired but a few minutes by the ocean and a few more gulps from mu giant coffee and I should be just fine."

"I don't want to find you out here still sleeping tomorrow morning."

"No, of course not. I want to sleep in my own bed tonight," Ari replies, a wistful stream of longing passing through him. "Officer Cameron. You know. That's the name of my dean over at the school."

"I know. That's my dad," he says, revealing an evident shift in tone as if he had standing ready to drop some of his professional stiffness. "I know who you are, Mr. Fisher."

"Really?"

"Sure."

"Well if Bud says so, it's all true," Ari says, attempting affability. He feels his sweat streaming once more from beneath his matted hair.

"I might take a class or two over there, to help me to ease my way into the university."

"Oh," Ari says. Relax. "Great. What would you like to do?"

"Get into law school one day."

"A cop and a lawyer. You could run for office on that ticket."

"Maybe. I've thought about that, too."

"I'll bet you do it, too. How long have you been a cop?"

"I'm going on my third year. Anyway, I'll do my undergrad in business. Dad told me I should definitely take your classes."

"That's...that's really great to hear. He said that?"

"Oh yeah. He's told me a couple of times, maybe forgetting himself. He was complaining about some of his other instructors. Headaches. Said he wished they were all like Fisher. "

"Well. I'm always glad to hear it." Ari feels dizzy. Then again, Cameron's criticism of Ari never had anything to do with his teaching.

"Yeah... we all need to hear that once in a while don't we," the young cop says, sounding oddly sad. "Mr. Fisher. Back to why we're here. I strongly encourage you to get some rest. Pull over there if you want to. But drive home safely."

"Of course."

"Mr. Fisher," Officer Cameron repeats, leveling him a look. "I will be personally very disappointed if I hear that you've been picked up later on for drunk driving or worse, if you get into an accident."

"So will I, young man. I mean, officer. So will I."

"Do you understand what I'm saying to you, Mr. Fisher?"

Ari peers again into young Cameron's face, though it's shrouded inside his helmet and in the shadow opposite the light. He can see the young, sensuous lips. But not the man's eyes. "Yes," Ari replies. "I understand." The cop completes the ticket, obtains Ari's signature.

"Get some rest. No more to drink tonight."

"God, no."

"No need to swear, Mr. Fisher." Ari smirks, but Cameron's head and helmet were lowered over his ticket book. The cop raises his head again. "You can go now. Be safe."

"Thank you...thank you. Good night, officer."

Officer Cameron turns around, boots scratching through the dirt. Ari sighs. The cop back and cocks his head at something. "Mr. Fisher."

"Yes."

"I notice your trunk is open."

"What?"

"Your trunk. It's open. I mean it's down, of course, but it wasn't locked." And then Officer Cameron leans over and opens the trunk. Ari's heart leaps into his gorge, his mouth opens and nothing comes out. The cop pushes it down again with a slam, then checks the edge of the trunk door to ensure that it's locked.

"Damn," Ari says. "I remember closing the trunk."

"It works fine," says Officer Cameron. "That won't need fixing."

"Ah. Good. Thank goodness for that."

"What you got in there?" He imagines the cop winking at him.

"Oh. Old linens. You know. Old linens. And clothes and blankets I'm gonna get rid of. Someday," Ari adds, lest the cop somehow imagine he intended to dump these items tonight.

"Spring cleaning."

"You said it. It's out of my house. Now I just need to get it out of my car."

"Who you giving it to?"

"Excuse me?"

"Have you figured out where to drop it off?"

"Oh. Salvation Army. Something like that."

"Yeah, there's one in Eureka. Kind a far. You know…I'm actually co-leading a community effort to collect blankets and clothing for the homeless and for needy families. Other necessities, too. We've got more folks on the street in these parts then people realize."

"That's awesome," Ari declares, aware of using a word he loathes as hyper inflated and misused amongst so many of his students. "Another reason why you'll one day be a Senator."

"I'm just doing it because it's the right thing to do," the cop says with efficient lack of humor. "How long have you had that bag in your trunk?"

"Only… a couple, two or three days, I think."

"How'd you like me to take it off your hands right now?"

105

"You're kidding?"

"No, I'm not. The collection point is behind the station in Arcata. Save you a trip."

"It's no problem. I drive it every day to work."

"Yeah, but the semester's over now."

"Well of course it is, but I still have to go down to the office to wrap things up, you know."

Officer Cameron taps his helmet with his flashlight. "Actually, I probably shouldn't be loading my own squad trunk with some bag like that." He looks at the trunk. Ari imagines the cop is debating whether to ask to inspect the contents.

Ari's opens his mouth to speak, his throat sore with dry. His tongue feels dusty and he tries to suck some sputum together in order to speak. He says, "You know, Arcata is much closer to me than Eureka, of course. How about you give me the address of the drop off so I can bring it down myself next week."

The cop taps his head again. He turns to Ari to look at him, but Ari cannot see his face, his figure illuminated only from the sides and the back, the nimbus of mechanical light splayed at his sides. "Just bring that bag to the station, Mr. Fisher." It sounded like a sullen command. Ari has visions of arriving at the collection point, grinning, winking, waving out the window, honking his horn, high fiving the mystified reception staff, the trunk yawning wide open at the touch of his remote. He hauls out the green bag, exhaling now its breath of the crypt, of soured coital juices, pungent neglect, the sagging, beaten linens fall away and there he presents his gangrene gargoyle, his mutant rabid bat monkey, his escapee from the coffin with its rusted, tetanus nails.

"OK," Ari tells the cop. "I'm leaving tomorrow out of town but I'll be back Wednesday."

"That's fine. Whatever you want to do."

Ari coughs. "Anything else, officer?"

"Get some rest. Drive safely. Don't get pulled over again."

∞

Three forty seven. Ari staggers back to the road. His car is nowhere in sight. It was here that he had decided to sit down, huddled up by a tree. He shuts his dry and swollen eyes for he was on the verge of finally passing out. Finally, he surrenders himself to leave his mind and to let his body be still. But the universe continues to spin, the more violently behind his eyelids. He sits, sore, pebbly scree, lumpy earth; he snorts himself awake from a phantom skirt of a dream, looking at the dark, slipping back into unknowing, heavy limbed dreamless torpor.

Officer Cameron in his mind's eye is still walking away. Ari is left alone with the ocean and his rotten cargo. He remembers now so long ago it seems, the moment when the cop's taillights disappeared over the ridge from which he came. At last, Ari was alone again. He crosses the street and he stands there listening, imagining the basalt waves that he cannot see, letting himself be momentarily held. Time to move on.

Finishing his convenience store coffee to its silty bottom, he navigated the black road towards Crescent City, taking care to respect the viperous blue fog, especially where the road hugs the sharpened cliffs, vigilant lest he follow little Leon Ng into the black and onto the rocks.

Highway 198 passes through the Jedediah Woods and continues inland, away from the enchanted coast and into the sun pan of the California interior. His intention was to drive as far as the arid flat lands eastward, yet twenty minutes inward he realized he would never make it before the sun was high in the sky. Ari was moreover down to a quarter tankful of gas. Just enough to make it back into town. So he slowed down, knowing that it was the forest indeed where he would have to find a way to disappear the contents of car.

In a wall of milk dissipated, in a narrow section of curving road, Ari pierces the veil of fog long enough to spot a dirt fire road. He pulled over, checking for signs that this was a private road. Satisfied that it was public land, Ari decided that this was the place. He turned and slowly drove, crunching over gravel, bumping over ruts deepened by dwarfed monsters of lingering tree roots. The road wound upwards, peering out for a quick turnout. And then, as if for the first time ever, the crystalabra of urgent and infinitely distant and numerous stars exploded into sight, the obscene and ubiquitous firmament. The fog is gone and from nowhere can it overcome this overwhelming evidence of the abyss and its retinue of vertigo. Here, in this place he would soon complete his errand. Because he had to.

The road became overgrown with high grass in its middle course, hissing as it disappears and thrashing beneath his car in its snaky whisper. Low branches tickle and knock against his windshield. And though he felt himself tighten, clenching his jaw against the danger of puncturing his tires or even collapsing off a cliff, he also held hope that this neglected patch of grit road led directly to a suitable final burial for his burdens. Another quarter mile or so of slow ambling, his car rocking over the rutted path.

In no particular place, Ari cut the engine. And the lights. At the first moment, the dark descended in total like a cloak. He sat in silence, rolled down the windows, which sounded oddly loud, the mechanical whirl breaking in his ears. The call of cicadas rose from a murmur to fill the void of sound. He gazed again up at the Milky Way splashed in back of a narrow vault of simmering stars overhead, his peripheral vision cut short by the stalks of skeletal trees rising like sentinels. He breathed and felt keen and ready. He would not have to travel far. The cicada chorus filled the sky.

He had no flashlight save for the one on his key ring. He was poorly prepared, he considered, to bury a body. Perhaps it was best this way, no light from his car or a torch to baldly announce his suspect skulking in the well of the wilderness. It would have to do, a narrow precious thread illuminating disjointed images of earth, ancient redwood needles, pebbles, bases of massive fallen trees, their veins of roots disrupting the ground. He opens the trunk and reaches inside it for his bag of supposed tree trimmings. As he hefted it, it was heavier than he expected. His hearted felt folded, ready to decline then explode from his chest. Poor Mrs. Ng. She deserved better, after all. Anyone would. Was it still possible to redeem any part of this mess? Was she not long dead, evacuated from her dry, leathery tomb? What an insult. No burial. He set the bag down, deciding he must drag it. He lurched back to the car to retrieve the final item, also deathly heavy, from beneath the bag. His garden shovel. Ari strained to drag both bag and shovel forward.

After a quarter mile or so into the woods themselves, away from the road, his key light revealed the hollow of a massive tree. Suddenly, Ari started to cry, tears without sentiment. He decided he was about to dump what used to be a life in a shallow grave beneath the tree, wrapped in sweaty cum soaked sheets inside a garbage bag. A stone hand.

He thinks; the coldest, most implacable serial killer could not have devised a more contemptible, uncaring way to dispose of a body. Ari held the bag from the bottom and the top to keep it from tearing, trembling as he sought to grasp the places where the linens were the thickest, hands fleeing from the least insinuation of an abandoned person lost within. If there is a Hell, I am going. Slowly, slowly, he crept further out into the forest, imagining his ankle twisting, his face tangled in a dumb branch, the bag breaking or worse, leaking, himself stepping into an incline, a ditch, or off a cliff.

With each studied uncertain step, he felt his determination grimly resurrecting. Just a few more feet. A few more feet and he would surely feel the perfect spot. Where she - where it – would never be found. A few more feet he chanted within, labored breaths, hauling his unholy loads, grasping hold on the his key light, radiating the tiny shaft of light upon the harrowing yet protective darkness that welcomed him, perhaps far too covetously.

Trying to manipulate the key chain, he dropped it into the silence. Ari blurted out, suppressing a stream of curses. He looked down, but of course he saw nothing at all. He lowered himself on his hands and knees to search the hungry forest floor. In the dark, he patted the dampened earth. Slowly he crawled all around the bag itself, crawling around the bag of bones in wider circles in the dark. Knowing that he might be paralyzed out here with no conceivable way of explaining himself, were he ever found, presuming he even survived. That's a fine way for my son to remember me. Some schmuck dead in the forest with a dead body in a hefty bag! Crawling. Look beneath the bag, he reluctantly instructed himself. Slowly, Ari inched back in the bag's supposed direction. He came upon it and lifted it, his hand upon a broken wing, an elbow. Then he heard them. The keys. A clink. He put his hands out, supplicating the earth, finally placing his left hand upon their cold and jagged edges. Instinctively, Ari thanked God, knowing again full well in almost the same moment that no such God as could possibly exist could ever welcome thanks for supposedly helping him to find his keys beneath a corpse in a bag that he had come to dump. Ari looped his finger inside the key ring, pressed down the button on the light, clutched the bag in one hand, found the shovel with the other. Pressed on.

No more than twenty paces further on, Ari found what he was looking for, another hollowed out tree, a two headed monster, trunks separating only as they climb eight or ten feet above the ground. Ari picked his way over its roots and into the blackened hollow, he laid the bag down. To his delight, it fell away out of sight almost immediately. He heard a soft thud, but only a brief moment. And now he would shovel in only that which was above the earth, leaves and bracken and twigs, so that he might in no way call attention to Mrs. Ng's final resting place.

At last he finds the dirt road. No twisting of limbs. No losing of keys. But where is his car? It begins to rain. He stands dripping, keys and shovel in hand. He turns around in the opposite direction to where he assumed he was supposed to look. There is only one dirt road, passable by car, the same tall grass and rutted knots. This must be it. Which way? The rain beats down, large marble drops, and it occurs to him that he had marched downward towards the hollow. He follows hopefully in the upward direction, squishing his shoes in the sudden mud. In the dim blue pre-dawn light he finds it, his car. Once again, Ari is granted the chance to survive.

Soon he will wash away the grave and the dead from him. He will have to get rid of his clothes as well. Maybe to the Salvation Army! He craved a dreamless sleep where the dead and the missing did not cry out to him. He nearly stumbles over the suitcase, nearly topples over. Ari curses but picks up the valise, and he thrashes out to the embankment on other side where there is a steep drop into the undisturbed forest in a waterless gorge below. Exhausted, Ari lets the valise fall into the tree tops, hopefully to burst open into blameless trash carried to the four corners by curious critters. Immediately after doing so, he instantly regrets his action and curses himself for now he will certainly be discovered and he finds that he barely gives a damn, only he will first complete his task because he simply must, even if all has become utterly futile. All he cares about now is getting home and getting to sleep.

Once inside the car, he watches for a moment the chaos upon his windshield. The sky lights up with a distant stroke of lightning. Ari turns the key but at first the engine fails to turn. Sweat pours from his temples, mixing with rainwater and he forces himself to give it time between attempts. On the third try the engine roars into life. The wheels spin at first without moving the car. Ari presses the gas and the car lurches forward, but nearly off the road, and he turns the wheels and tediously three points the vehicle to turn it around in its narrow enclave. He straightens out determined to find a gas station and a bed. Maybe a drink. Ha!

Slowly he edges his way down the congealing dirt road, the rain obscuring his vision, arboreal sentries looming in his high beams. At last he reaches the road and he calculates to turn right, towards Crescent City. The warning light on his gas gauge flashes alive, but he expects he'll have enough to make it.

The town is dead enough when he arrives, ensconced in a blue gray early dawn of fog. There were no gas stations open that he could find and he has to pull over soon. Perversely, he knows where he will go, though it's stupid and unnecessary. But it is familiar, even if it's

111

horrible. Now he seeks comfort in going there, the place where he least wanted to go.

Despite the rain, Ari parks two blocks away from the Sea View Motel, as if to protect his anonymity somehow. The Sea View is an eight room, white stucco inn, discarded construction tools and beer cans in its paltry back property, an unkempt lawn up front and frequented by day laborers sharing a room, the occasional transient family without a trailer, smelling of greasy cooking, and the goblin professionals who rent in cash by the hour. There was also the occasional solo occupant whose sole occupations were drinking, smoking, and hazy versions of sleep, with no apparent intention of living or dying. Barren, peeling rooms, threadbare linens, brooding dark green walls, cleaned only when occupants drifted on. Never would he have chosen such a place to take her. She led him here, whether she meant to or not.

The street was unlit, the fog and mist hovering still. Ari walks the middle of the street, hands in pocket, second guessing his decision to park at a distance. (How could two blocks fool the police if they were looking for him?) The motel was illuminated by a single street lamp. Its little office faces the tiny weed choked construction yard, away from him. He shocks to a sudden stop at a monolith like being he had never seen before.

"Hey brother," it said. "I don't mean you no harm and no offense, and I don't want nothing from you. You hear me?"

"What?" was all that Ari could eke out. He looks back in the blue gray darkness towards his car. Both of them stand in the softening rain.

"Brother. I don't want to drink no more. I don't want to use no more. I don't want to hurt or hurt nobody no more. You understand?" Peaceful words, but they sounded like a threat to Ari. The man, large, bulky, with a scraggly beard and long stringy hair, emerges dimly, but Ari still cannot make out the face. He resented the man's presence.

"Good for you, man. Have a good night."

"Look!" the man shouts and steps forward into the halogen light. His eyes seem to vibrate and his face looks darkened, weathered by prolonged exposure outdoors. "I don't do something for nothing. I'm about to drink. Understand? And if I do that, it's no good for me, and I'm telling you, it'll be no good for you neither."

"What do you want, then?"

"Just this," he bellows. "I can't get rid of it myself. I found it in my bag, in my room. I thought I was rid of it. I thought it was all gone. If you'd a come twenty seconds later I would a drank it. And then all hell would a broke loose. I can't smash it. I can't do it. I can't drink it. It's not even broken, man. Just take the goddamn thing. Please!"

Ari stares recoiling, dumbstruck. "What?"

"What?" the man repeats. "Take the goddamn bottle is all. Drink it. Or smash it for me. So I don't get smashed, man, or so I don't smash it against your head man, man. Fuckin' listen to me."

"Fine. Alright. I can take it!" Ari says. A light flicks on in the office. "Where is it? Hold it out."

The man does so. His shoulders seemed to soften. "Here," he says quietly, and he holds the bottle outstretched.

Ari's legs stiffen, but then he warily steps forward, gingerly puts out his hand, says, "So you want me to take it?"

"Take it now," the man hoarsely calls. "Take it, damnit."

The man holds the base so Ari grabs the neck and pulls it away, half expecting the man to punch him. It surprises him to feel the heft of the bottle. In the light from the office, Ari can see that it's fifth of some no-name vodka or gin. He steps back and feels the neck. Indeed the seal feels as if it has never been broken.

"Brand new bottle."

"God has sent you to me," the man says.

"What?"

"I would a drank. I would a killed someone."

"Alright…..thanks for the bottle. Be safe. I'm going to bed." Ari turns to dash for the dubious safety of the front office. Or maybe I'll just run like hell back to my car, swinging the bottle.

"Hey," the man shouts.

Ari freezes. "What!"

"Give me some money."

"Money!"

"I said you gotta hearing problem"

"What about it. You were just going to smash it."

"I need a place to sleep. You got yourself a brand new bottle. Give me the fuckin' money."

Ari imagines smashing the bottle in the man's unseen face but even in his imagination, he is weak and ineffectual. The bottle would only tap unbroken against this monster. "I don't have time for this," he mutters instead, a man who just buried a corpse of a woman with whom he had had inappropriate drunken, sex. "You mind if I put the bottle down?"

"It's your bottle."

Ari does so and opens his wallet, fingering a twenty dollar bill and holding it out stiffly with two fingers. He wonders that there is so much cash in his wallet, a neat band of twenties. "That's twenty."

The man emerges, half of his strange face briefly revealed in the sickly light. Ari never sees the hand that snatches the twenty from his hand, a calloused mitt of a great hand. The man passes within breathing distance of Ari, the hairs on Ari's neck burning. "You're lucky I don't need more," is what the man whispers, and he bumps Ari's shoulder and massively glides on, without another word, crossing the blackened street, disappearing down the way Ari came, a moment later swallowed by the mists. Ari stands, clutching his bottle.

He turns to the office, hides the bottle and walks around, opening the narrow door. A frightened looking East Indian man, with unnaturally light patchy skin, a likely burn survivor, blinks at him. Ari asks for a room.

"Who were you talking to out there?" the man asks in his musical, clipped accent.

"Who? I don't know who that was. A vagrant."

"You shouldn't be out like this and talking to men like that. Not you."

"Pardon me."

"Room seven."

"Really? Room seven?"

"Room seven we have available for you. But not for him."

"Of course it is just for me."

"How long are you staying?"

"Until I get a good night's sleep."

"Check out is at eleven. I'm sorry, but if you stay past that I still have to charge you for another night."

"I don't care. What time is it?"

"Just after five. Here you are," the man says handing him an old fashioned metal key attached to a white plastic card with the number seven on it.

"Not very secure is it, when your room number is on this."

"What do you mean? Is very secure."

"Just kidding."

"Just don't lose your key, between here. And there." He gestures sardonically. "And no smoking inside the room itself. That's the only rule."

"That's a promise.

Ari bolts the door and lowers the shade. He turns on the heater, hoping for a leaven of white spacious sound. Instead, the system roars into place like the grinding of gears. He takes of his wet jacket and his muddy shoes and he lies on the creaky thin bed with its fungal smelling sheets. The walls are painted a deep, lonely green, bare except for a mocking twelve inch still life of a heaping plate of waxy fruit, throbbing against a black, funereal background. Grapes and pears and cherries at rest at night.

Why am I here? Because I can't take another minute of driving and I have no more gas in my car and I must simply and finally pass out. But why here! Why ultimately here in this shit hole and in this particular goddamn room, haunted by ghosts. I am here because I wanted it to be here. Not home. But here. It's what I wanted. Shit.

He breaks the seal on the bottle and takes a swallow directly – thank you for the drink! He seeks an absolute guarantee of oblivion. At the second pull of vodka, Ari feels the heat and glow from the alcohol. On his third drink, it occurs to him that this might be the one place, ironically, where he might be most free from Mrs. Ng.

115

Suddenly, Ari touches a hidden well spring of grief, oozing from the desolate walls of this loveless room. This sludge of loss and futility may or may not have anything to do with his neglected lover. He takes a fourth pull from the crazy man's bottle. The sadness cozies up and tingles through him. Through that door she had disappeared, even though he had expected that she would return almost immediately, as she always had. But then she was gone.

He sits up or imagines that he has done so. The little wooden chair is still there, heavier and darker than he remembers. This was where he had first found her in this room, looking down, hands on her legs. Ari takes a fifth drink, then puts the bottle down on the chair itself and he stumbles to his feet and glowers down at the chair, prepared to call Jasmine to account, talking to the bottle in absentia, a pathetic yet beloved little avatar. The room threatens to spin and once it starts he knows he won't be able to stop it, no matter how much he remembers.

A text had arrived, the day after an insane fight, fueled by sarcasm and mutual self-loathing. "We need to talk. Now." He ignored her. She texted again. Exclamation marks. Finally the new message. "I'm pregnant."

He called her. Maybe it was a sick joke. A way of getting attention or upsetting him or both. But he knew it was neither. Irresponsible, rambunctious tryst. Inconsistent precautions, actions spoken, not taken, resolutions rising and dissipating like steam. "I'd like to just have this baby with you," she said as if waking from a nap, "And to live in your magic house in your enchanted fucking forest and to just be normal, to be a mom, and to enjoy life. I want to do all that except there's just one small tiny little thing. I hate your guts. I hate your guts Ari and I hate everything about you and I would hate this baby, too, and everything about my life, and you'd probably just hide me there like a prisoner or forget about me altogether and you'd just want to kill this baby all the time and so would I, and you'd want to kill me, too, and you're dead deep inside anyway. And that's the real reason I hate you. I hate you because of how much you hate me."

"Enough, Jasmine. That's enough. Where are you right now?"

"My ghost is going to haunt you."

"Goddamn it. Where are you?"

"Mr. Fisher," she said, which she often called him in public and even mockingly in private. She called me Mr. Fisher. He had nothing to say and he did feel dead inside and he was about to make up something when the door banged and banged in extremis. Sheriff? Vice squad? FBI? Bud Cameron?

"Open your door, Ari. You wanted to know where I am." Ari threw down the phone and though he felt a shaft of fear searing through him, he called out to her and he threw open the door and he was struck anew by how small and how puny she looked. And she leaned into his arms and he held her there and finally there was a moment of peace, softness and a quiet had at long last arrived.

But it didn't last long. Time kept on. What now? Peace could only remain if she simply evaporated and returned in his dreams, forever naked and nineteen, right here, in a parallel dream house of his own. Of course he was willfully forgetting something, obvious and glaring. He was forgetting absolutely everything. It was she who spoke of it. Ari knew at that moment he was but a mere boy, fitted inside a hairy, full sized man's body and it disgusted him and he pushed the thought away but now he could push no further what this girl was saying. Impossible. She was talking of keeping the baby. If only to keep him?

Back in the present moment, lost in its vodka haze and sleepless stupor, Ari upends the bottle. Less than half full now, a few precious drops dribbling down his chin. Ah yes, one more member of Mrs. Ng's illustrious lineage that he has personally destroyed, including herself. Yes indeed. Sorry, so sorry about that. Sabrina asks him again. Why are you sorry? I'm sorry because that's all I can say or do. They came with treasure, love, pleasure, and he killed them all with carelessness. You and your grandson, dead. Your granddaughter, wandering through her unknown perdition, and your great grandchild, Ari was certain, will never be born. Too bad I missed a generation. How sloppy I am. Jasmine's melancholy mother. He laughs out loud, a clumsy, ugly sound, still wondering behind his disembodied haze, a curious ember, wondering if he could still be human. How much easier it would be if he were not. If only he were never more human.

So many times before she had proven to him that she could appear and disappear at any moment. She could level him with a dark look, a whip of her head, a matted lock of hair; and in the very seem instant it seemed, Jasmine would grab her shoes and flee in less time than it took for Ari to fully accept that she was leaving. Go on, he would think. Leave and don't come back, only to long for her within in minutes.

Of course he knew what he had said and done, and what he had left unsaid and undone. He knew exactly why she left him and without a trace. I'm keeping the baby, so she said. What? She was moving in. Really. When? For the first time he took note of her stuffed and rumpled duffle bag. She was here. Had he ever told her, No you're not? He had not. He never told her to get rid of this thing. (The baby) Never used the "A" word. So what was it? He opens the bottle and takes a ninth pull and a tenth pull, it contents getting dangerously low. The room begins to pulse and glow, faster and hotter, Ari feeling feverish while sitting in his wet and pasted clothing. Of course he knew what he had done.

Ari laughed at her.

It wasn't much. It was unapologetic. No apparent sense of self-deprecation that either one of them could detect, not much that could be misunderstood. Laughter; spontaneous and malicious. He had laughed and squeezed his eyes shut and shook his head which he held in his trembling hands. He laughed.

So she fled.

The door slammed. He rubbed his temples, waiting to hear the presumptuous knocking on his door. Nothing. Yes, in a few minutes she would be back. And there was the proof, right there. Her duffle bag. Exactly where she had dropped it. Excellent. I will walk outside and find you sitting on my door step, bent over, crying. Waiting. Hoping I will burst outside, panicked, chagrinned, shouting, shouting your name. Oh God! There you are, baby. Baby, come inside. We're gonna figure this out. We'll do it together. Together. (Fuck you!) So here I come!

But there is only the drizzle and the travelling, soundless fog, passing at close range. No Jasmine. He calls out. He shouts her name. He asks her to come back inside. No one.

Ari now stands and places the bottle back on the chair and he shakes his head and he looks at the little bottle and he feels so sad, for Jasmine is so very small. You did not have to leave. But didn't she? Well I could not just let her leave. So I did the right thing, didn't I? I went after her. His car never wanted to be disturbed, but finally it roared into gear, coming to life and emerging from his lair, its lights ablaze.

He had tried to calm himself, shaking his head at the absurdity of chasing her down the frontage road where she would surely have been stuck for hours without a ride. But he was wrong. Ari drove up and down in both directions, north and south, seeing no one. Could she have possibly disappeared down the pathway towards the gravel windy beach itself, mincing across the rocky shoals, pebbles and petrified wood. He decided to rule this out and he headed north again.

She had hinted she had friends to the north. There was nothing for her southward but her empty rented room. He called her on her cell. He texted her. "Where r u? I want 2 c u. I'm in my car looking 4 u." Twice he pulled over where the road met the ocean front. Nothing but its leaden waves. The hell with her. But he kept on. Of course, the only way she could have come any distance at all was that she had actually caught a ride after all. She had done it before, many times - to see him - risking rape and kidnapping at the hands of a merciless loony. The thought horrified him, but it also made him oddly jealous, as if she'd enthusiastically fellate some freak just to get a ride to see Ari, her lover. I love you so much that I gave this guy the best head of his life. Was that what she was up to right now? The thought of it angered him. And aroused him as well. He knew he was inane yet he was still thoroughly entangled in such knotted thoughts as he turned a curve and saw Jasmine waiting there as he entered the splendid valley that heralded the dubious hamlet of Orrick.

He was so awakened by the bejeweled beauty of the land that he nearly missed spotting her, wrapping herself in her arms inside her fleece sweater and her thrift store knit cap, shivering by the side of the road,

119

thumb defiantly out. He had already passed her and was looking for a place to pull over on a shoulder by some tall grass just before the village limits, next to an abandoned gas station, not far from the first of Orick's several maddening Burl shops, enchanted by its incomprehensible wooden elementals and twisted knick-knacks.

Ari waited, turning off the engine, watching her struggle alone, waiting for her to notice and to blithely come and enter his car. With relief he noted that no one could know that beneath that lumpy bundle at the side of the road there writhed a sinewy wild child; precious, insane, dysfunctionally brilliant, endlessly exasperating and ever intoxicating. Yes, she would come to him now, like a chastened little girl, ruefully done with her tantrum, duly diminished and abashed. Yes, she would come to him and the first thing she would say to him would be, "I'm hungry."

And what could possibly come after that? Was it their destiny to make a future, to make a life with each other because they had carelessly created something far more important than anything that could have ever happened otherwise between them? Would they tame each other into mutual, shared respect and deference, bearing their burdens together, crashing into creation, into family? Or would he instead seek treatment for her and a loving, vetted family for their unborn son or daughter? More than likely, of course - inevitably - he was here and he knew he was here so that they might ready themselves to chase each other down a far more narrow and darker alley, still?

While still sorting out these possibilities, imagining himself dragging her directly to the abortion clinic, a blue pick-up truck slowed down in his rear view mirror, over to where the girl still, stomping her feet for warmth. Without so much as talking to the driver or peeking inside, she quickly stepped up into the passenger seat, slamming the door, disappearing inside. And the truck pulls out and away and in the next second passes within two or three feet of Ari's car. He sits for a moment, utterly dumbstruck. At last he fumbles for his keys to follow her, slanting past Orick, piling further north.

120

It wasn't so hard to follow. He doesn't like the looks of the truck, navy blue, shiny, maybe a Ford 150, exuding lust and avarice in its unnecessary power, salivating at his fucked up little Jasmine. He was able to follow at an estimated fifteen to twenty lengths, no signs of evasive action, no brusque pulls to the side of the lonely road, no invitation to confront an uninhibited, steely muscled hot head, easy grip upon his tire iron, bracing to wield it crashing through Ari's windshield, before hoisting Ari himself, crumpled and scraping from the car before smashing the iron across his face and through his skull, foreplay to the madman's raping Jasmine before Ari's dimming, blood soaked eyes. Ari grips the wheel, fuming at the realization that he is not in the least bit control of this situation.

Then again, what would you do even if you had her back in your car, safe and secure for the briefest of moments? What was there to change? Turn around. Go home. Now!

Instead, Ari continue instead to follow hunched against the wheel, curving against the treacherous ocean cliffs that open upon sudden panoramic views of misted the forest.

When the truck pulled over at a gas station, both driver and passenger stepped out. The driver indeed was male and muscular, but short, a young man in a brilliant white t-shirt. When he stepped out to conduct his business, he acted as if he was alone and had been so the whole time, completely oblivious of his passenger. Jasmine slowly dragged herself into the convenience store. Ari pulled over to the sidewalk, straining himself to scan the entrance of the mini mart. When Jasmine re-emerged, carrying a small plastic bag, she headed not back to the car but up the street away from the main road, away from the driver. Ari pulled slowly out to follow her. He could have easily overtaken her and spoken to her from his car, but he chose instead to get out and follow her on foot to the motel. He watches her enter the office and he stops a moment, waiting for her to re-emerge a few minutes later. Ari approaches until he is close enough to see her come out again and enter a room on the far end of the squalid little property.

121

Mist and fog. The door and its knob were wet, slippery. This place looked like a place where one came when one had nothing to do, nothing to learn, nowhere to go, and no one to meet, at least no one you ever expected to see again. His knock was timid. After all this crap, he wondered if he wanted to even be here.

He heard a light movement. The door stirred and she opened it without asking who it was and without visibly registering the least surprise or any other emotion. It was Ari who gasped in surprise, suddenly amazed that he had actually tracked her down. She turned away from him without a word and she walked with indifference to the wooden chair beside the bed. At last she had taken off that silly cap and jacket. She sat there mute, remote, sitting curiously straight, staring down at her hands upon her knees.

It was just this image of her that remains in his dreams of her, frozen she was in attentive resignation. Sometimes, this was all he dreamed, this very tableau, Jasmine sitting, eyes averted away, cross eyed, consternated. He'd see her in his dream, mute, voiceless, looming helplessly over her own invisible abyss.

In his memory, what he did next was take off his coat and lay it on the floor. He sat on the edge of the creaky bed, beside her. Where to start? Tears leaked from her otherwise impassive features. He spoke.

"Baby...baby, I'm so glad I found you. I didn't mean to push you away." She sniffed and continued to leak slowly from her eyes and from one of her nostrils. She was like a child, he thought. "Come back with me. OK?" Still, she said nothing. "Come on, sweetie," he continued, "Let's take this back to town. Stay with me tonight. And then we'll talk about what to do next."

Flatly, without looking up, she responded. "You've already decided."

"Why did you come here?" he asked.

She looked at him quizzically and explained as if it was an answer to the stupidest question possible. "Because I was tired."

"Come on, honey. Let's go."

"No."

"Let's go, Jasmine. This is no place for us."

"Why did you bring my duffle bag?"

"What?"

She looked at him levelly. "Why did you bring my duffle bag, Ari?"

He looked towards where he saw her eyes go. There it was near the door. He felt as if he had forgotten that he had ever carried the thing. "Jazz. What do you mean? Why wouldn't I bring it?"

Quietly, staring off, she said to him, "Don't you know? You're supposed to be smart."

"Obviously I brought it so you'd have your things, baby."

She turned to him again. "Because obviously it doesn't belong at your place, right?"

"What?"

"What are you, stupid, Ari? Which part of what I'm saying don't you understand?"

He stares back at her, feeling hot in his face. "I understand you're really upset and probably really, really scared."

"But you don't want my things stinking up your nice new sanitarium in the middle of your own little magical forest."

"Jazz," he whispered hoarsely. "Please. Just look at me."

"I am looking at you, Ari," and indeed she was, level, dry eyed.

"Well, I'm here now. Obviously. I mean, I didn't want you to go at all and I came after you. Yes?"

"You just didn't want me coming back for my stuff."

"Me *and* your stuff are both here now. And I'm not going anywhere."

She looked down and away, looking at her feet, and she softly observed. "You hate me, Ari."

"What?"

"You can't stand the sight of me."

An uninvited voice in his head suggested to him that this might be true. "How utterly ridiculous, Jasmine. And you know it. Now enough with the self-pity." She said nothing. "Come home with me."

"You sound so angry, Ari."

123

"I'm frustrated. Because I came all the way out here. Obviously I care about you."

"Obviously?"

"Jazz."

"You hate me," she said, quietly weeping. "You wish I was dead."

Maybe I do right now, just a little, he thought in a place he hoped he could hide. "Jazz. Baby. Let's go home now." Nothing. She said nothing. "Honey?"

"You talk to me like you're my dad. Who are you?"

"Jasmine. I want you to come back with me. Please."

"Why?" she asked, still looking down. "So you can throw me out later?"

"I never threw you out before. You ran away, baby. Remember?"

"So you can kill your own child?"

He hung his head and sighed. What could he do? I'm just a complete and utter schmuck. "I'm not going to argue. I just want you to come back with me. Please."

"I'm tired, Ari."

"Me too, baby."

"I wanna go to sleep."

"Here?"

"You can stay with me. I've already paid for the room."

"How did you do that?" he could not stop himself from asking.

"With your credit card."

"You had my card? And this is the dump you chose?" Of course he meant to be funny, but she just put her hands in her pockets and looked down again, wiggling her feet. It's as if she were offended because Ari did not appreciate her choice of motel. "Well there it is," he told her. "I'll stay with you, then."

She shrugged. "Do what you want?"

"Aren't you glad now I brought your bag?"

She smiled without looking at him and pushed up her glasses. "Would you do me a favor, if you could spare the time from your busy schedule?"

"What's that, baby?"

"Please bite me, Ari."

He smiled. "Anywhere you like, my dear."

Her smile faded, but she seemed subdued, softened now, eyes half closed. "Would you do me another favor? Before that."

"Yeah, pumpkin."

"Would you hold me?" she asked in a thin, little voice.

As she sits in the thin, little chair, he held his arms out to her, as he holds them out her now in his teetering acetone state, a supplicating gesture to his near empty Vodka bottle. "Cummere," he cooed to her back then, as he murmurs to her now, that sorrowful little bottle in the wooden chair.

"You come here," she whined.

"We won't fit there, baby." So he leaned towards her and cradling her shoulder gently lifted her to him and she fell, melting into his arms, limp and heavy. What now? And what am I doing and where are we going? To the abortionist? There on his last night with her safely in his embrace all he had in mind at that moment was to simply hold her still. But if his task had been to protect her, surely he had failed her miserably. For even at that moment he still really wanted to be elsewhere, convened within his splendid loneliness, perhaps in fact where he was right now, starting down at that empty chair, aghast at what he saw.

Jasmine raised her head, staring at him with bold yet sleepy, bloodshot eyes. And he kissed her and she latched on, a wild eely thing, and it was always like this, devouring each other in the void; clothing, inhibitions, compunctions all easily and violently discarded. It occurred to him that she was already pregnant and what was the harm or hurting of it and soon enough she erupted in that cry that boiled his blood and burst through his fingers. "Ooohhh!!" Simple. And on it went and he lost himself in her cries and her sweat the taste of warm seawater swarming with living things, and wave after wave of grasping, swimming and rocking, bedeviled in her rollicking war cry, "Ooooh!! Ooohh!!" And again she expelled her sorrow as he slaked his thirst and grew his claws.

"Noooh!! Nooooh!!"

Was it not her lead, her dance? Passion corrupted by terror. She chanted in rage and despair. "Noooh!! Nooh!!"

No! She told him. No.

Many ages it seemed, in a dream within a dream, Ari recalls a weak and smoky light penetrating through the blinds. He turns and crawls from one corner to the next, seeking the dark. He is stiff and cold, his head throbbing, stomach clenched, grateful to escape the light. Groping on elbows towards what must be the bed, Ari fumbles for something he cannot name, a primal memory. The bottle. Just enough he hopes. And then no more. He finds it, but knocks it over and when he can see he spies the last of it staining the carpet. Ari falls back, coughing, moaning mutely, and giving himself up to staring at the void in the unloved ceiling, rivers of cracks, dense queues of refugee ants at their edges.

Ari drifts in and out of the moment. He tries to rise up, his head evaporating, the room disintegrating. For a moment, he expects he will fall and he doesn't care, but then his sight and his sense returns somehow and he staggers into the little bathroom to imperfectly void himself. With unwanted clarity, Ari stares at the whiteness of the scrubbed baseboards, the chipped crumbs of paint and ancient tears of urine or more likely the leeched water from the algae stained roof.

She was holding herself when it was done and when he tried to touch her she recoiled and he could not see her eyes through her matted hair. Shaking her head. "I feel so empty."

"What?"

"This is all I'm ever good for."

"What?"

"Stop saying 'what'!"

126

"Don't say that. 'That's all I'm good for.'"

"Why not?" He had no answer. "You wanted this. Congratulations. But you don't want me."

"Damn it, Jasmine. Why are you saying that?"

Staring at nothing she tells him. "That's boring. You asking me that. You already know."

"I don't anything, Jasmine."

"There's nothing that comes after this. There's nothing that comes after this," she repeated. In their final coupling had she not so clearly wanted what he had also wanted? And yet it was mutely clear that this time around - if only this one time - she had expected him to catch her when she fell instead of falling with her or pushing her down. She had hoped that her man could be counted on to be her man, and more than just the sybaritic leper which in her eyes he had finally become, with nothing more to ever redeem him.

"Jasmine."

She sprang from her corner and stormed naked into the bathroom. He sat there not knowing, listening to the comforting sound of rushing hot water. When she came out she did not look at him and he felt stupid and he kept saying her name softly. Only once did she look at him - when she hoisted her duffle bag. Thanks for my bag, he imagined her saying, but she did not. The door closed behind her without a sound. This time he had no illusions about her coming back. Stupidly, he sat in the little room until he rose and drifted to the door and when he opened it and looked out he knew what he would find. Though she could not have been far, the fog had already swallowed her completely, whole and without a trace, as though she had ever existed. This time the wall of fog that met him there, though chimeric and illusory as always, spoke to him now in its language of stunning silence, lauding itself as immune to every challenge.

And now the fog tonight had returned him here, after all, disgorged and crouching in its lifeless amniotic embrace back inside this very place, as if he had never left and never could. Ari raises his head,

127

suddenly cut and wounded by a disgusting revelation. He had missed it. Simon's going away party.

Fuck Mrs. Ng. Fuck Bud Cameron. The hell with Jasmine, crazy wounded creature. He had just lost the only person in the world whom he truly loved and who loved him as well.

Fuck me!

His last conscious act was to shuffle like a shell shocked centenarian back into his stale and loveless bed. Ari remembered wishing, as if from the bottom of a well, the childish wish that he might somehow awaken far, far, away from here.

Fuck me, fuck me, he whispers, his mantra, fuck me, calm and slowly, fuck me, fuck me, he bides himself into forgetfulness, embracing the onset of oblivion.

When he opens his eyes again, his wish has come true.

In the interim he had imagined moments or centuries between the here and the there and the unconscious portion of the landscape he had wandered through since he did not know when. He had opened his eyes or thought he had, sometimes on the bed, sometimes arguing with the light, or negotiating with the dark, on the floor, standing, sitting, dreaming, babbling. Someone was so very very sorry and it irritated him greatly. Enough words. Who was it, where did that sorry ass, lewd, and shameful sobbing come from? Come now, we're strong again and we'll chase after lions and run against the moon, leaping from cliffs, the moon upon the waters as well as catapulted in the sky. Endless talking, soothing, negotiating, groping about in the bright lingering mists of limbo, until finally, a splice of pure and untimed annihilation.

So at last he opens his eyes and remembers nothing of this.

All is at last quiet and at peace. He is cold and full of ache and his eyes are swollen and he cannot keep them open at first. He practices opening and closing them just to see if he would get the same result, first to know that he is still alive, and then that he is awake.

The room is gone. In its place he cannot be sure at first, but then all at once he realizes he is sitting safely in his car. A mottled jumble of blurry light and shade beyond his windshield fails to resolve itself. The

128

car is not moving. It smells of stale water and cracked leather. He opens the driver door and looks at the pavement and it dawns on him that he is parked perfectly safe and straight in an empty lot in a familiar place. It is daylight, but it is hard to know whether morning or afternoon for the chalky white sky mutes any such judgment. Ari watches the trees all around him and he guesses exactly where he is, though he still cannot trust as yet than any of it is real.

The air rushing in from the open door is bone chilly and the sky is distant and clear of mists, remote with the hue of bones as well as chalk. Ari closes the door and rolls down the window and he feels a loneliness such as he has never known.

He knows this place very well. This is the lot for the Redwood Trail, though there were many others further up the nearby road. How he had arrived in one piece, driving in a pure and total black out is beyond all merit and understanding. It just is. The boy whose name he can no longer recall, the one who crashed his car over the cliffs, had he not been sober and in his right mind when he lost his life? How have I not awakened dead, drowned, slammed into a tree, or worse yet, crunching horrifically over little children? Maybe I have!

Ari opens the door feeling puny and stiff. Putting his feet to the ground, he finds himself barefoot but otherwise fully clothed. Gingerly, Ari braves the cold and the scabrous cement and he anxiously checks his bumper for dents, for broken lights and fenders, for blood and sinew. He checks the tires and walks slowly around the entire car. The car is unblemished except for mud streaks above his tires and below the doors, grime grimly acquired from his crime.

He remembers the walking shoes he had always kept in the backseat along with a pair of dry socks. His shirt is damp, smelling of bile, and is ruined. It was more than likely infected with Mrs. Ng's outraged DNA. He shivers and remembers that there might be a sweatshirt in the trunk. He opens it. Revolted, Ari searches inside his erstwhile sarcophagus. The only traces of mayhem are a few dark crumbs of soil and dried needles. Stray shards of green plastic still haunt the site as well. Nothing more. A faint whiff of motor oil. No discernible traces of blood or bone, but he can't be sure and he reaches for his crumpled sweatshirt, cringing in the corner, hiding behind old binders, textbooks, and magazines, as if it too were still appalled by the dead and the insulted.

Knowing that he has driven himself here in a black out, he feels vastly inferior to the workings of his subconscious and so he continues to feel clueless as to how it could have happened. Ari decides to accept the completely unreasonable theory which presented itself. He is meant to be here.

Ignoring his thirst, he enters, glancing at the signs that warn of black bears and the map of the trail. He feels clumsy and stiff, delivered unready from his wiser black out avatar. As he takes his first unsteady steps, a very light wind momentarily wafts through the tree tops, and a weak strand of fog seems to recede away from him.

The trail is flat, threading through glades, suddenly overlooking clearings of open fields and hills before disappearing for good into the shadow of the forest, narrow thread, lightly penetrating the hollow vigil of giants, light peering through its tops, trunks massive and other worldly. He passes by legions of luminous ferns and over tiny wooden bridges, unnecessary yet charming conveyances over muddy passes. On his right is a field of ferns surrounded by more distant, towering Brahmins, the sun itself weakly tries to wink through the fading mist.

He comes to fully accept that he is really here, and not still passed out at the motel or dead from choking on his own vomit, or wrapped around a tree, an axle steeped up was once his sphincter, blood cascaded from his surprised looking jaw, or perhaps instead ass naked licking the rancid inner wall of a dumpster in a Eureka alleyway, or possibly lying in his own puke, a curiosity at the Humboldt county jail, officer Cameron bemused and shaking his head, his father, Bud, the numbing effects of bafflement quickly giving way to silent yet apoplectic, purple rage - or perhaps and most likely of all possible universes, is the one where Ari is still weightless, still in midair, still sailing high above the ocean, he and his car, still gripping that steering wheel, barely a second before crashing upon the invisible rocks and into the boiling waves and the eternal silence that awaits him below.

None of that. He is here, unaccountably spared. He holds his hands in his pockets, chilled from the lingering damp and stupor. He wishes that he could just disappear into this enchanted where he could stay forever, doomed to suffer exquisite lonesomeness while yearning for something he can never name. A state of childlike madness. Perhaps approached by and cared for by elemental figures that wait upon him, the nymphs and elves and gnomes. His shoes upon the gentle earth and the sound of his own shallow breath are the only sounds.

Ari watches the trees, the earth, and the milky light as if for the first time, amazed, staring, as if disoriented by the patterns of legions of ferns or the gnarl and moss that hangs from fallen giants The low hanging mists recede from him as if coyly flirting and seducing him. Silent sirens seem to call, a glassy melody toying through his head. He crosses a foot bridge over a feeble gurgling stream, choked with mossy flora. More than once he stops to glance at finger length centipedes and mucous slathered banana slugs, each making their own labored progress towards their own inscrutable horizons. Cold and thirsty and tired as he is, he still keeps walking, not knowing what else to do, unable to go home it seems, for the house is surely haunted now, in any case. He can tell that he hasn't much further to go until he reaches the river. During the summer, the water is low enough that one can cross over the barren white stones to where the trail resumes. Passage was impossible now for the frequent rains.

There is a single wooden bench, bolted to the earth. Damp and cold, he sits and gazes out. Directly in front of him are rows of relatively puny, hundred foot pines. To his left, the foliage thins and shortens. A narrow clearing reveals a short but steep descent to the water's edge and a patch of sky. Ari carefully picks his way, kneels and washes his hands in the chilly flow, then scoops himself several gorgeous gulps of the river. Wiping his hands on his pants he returns to his bench and sits down facing the river. Silence.

He rubs his face and blinks. The wind picks up; the kind that often signals the rain. The sifting of wind in the tree tops fills the forest and his ears with a satiny shimmer and he wraps his arms around himself, deciding he will leave when the rain begins to fall, which they do not.

Instead, the day suddenly brightens and Ari looks up to see the clouds drifting and a vault of baby blue sky and the light of day expands over the river and even touches the ground where he sits, bathing it in gold, though it fails to warm his bones just yet. The day is bright and clear and Ari looks up at the sky again, the rare blue sky of May. For a long time he watches a bird, perhaps a hawk, outstretched wings, floating in the blue, circling higher and higher above, in slow, patient, yearning arches.

Simon Fisher feels his phone vibrating yet again inside coat pocket, but he ignores it for now. He knows who it is. Instead, he looks into his mother's sad and brave little smile, her big brown, limpid eyes. Some of his buddies had earlier remarked to his face that his mother was "hot". If they said nothing, he could still surmise what they were thinking by their embarrassed little smiles upon meeting her. All he could see of course was his mother, a being alien from all intemperate desire. In her lovely eyes he mostly witnessed the creases that separate women from girls, the faint touches of powder on her that to him registered shame instead of affirmation of the flesh, and the hardness that slowly crept into her hands, the raised veins, the liver spots. Yet she still looked amazing in blue jeans and a sweater, or so he was told.

What he would miss in saying goodbye was the knowledge that she was there, that he could ask her for anything, even if the answer was no. But all he wanted at that moment was to give her that final awkward hug and kiss and to be on his way through security, alone, breathing easily. Before engaging his travelling cohort at the gate, he would have no problem checking his phone, but not before that.

They were not alone, mother and son. His longtime friend and hiking companion, Nigel, remained, as well as his sullen on again, off again girlfriend, Kelley, who though she had insisted on coming now looked like she would prefer to be anywhere else in the world but right here. Simon was grateful that Paul had not come, apparently taking the hint that he was not welcomed. Simon was disgusted with Paul, but it was so much easier of course to loathe such a man than to take it out on his own mother - or father - for fucking up and collapsing the marriage. As a young teen, he would throw his friends a corner smile when they remarked on his mother's good looks, but now he no longer tolerated it, and his companions understood.

At last come the awkward goodbyes, the shoulder hug with Nigel and their clashing palms in a manly tennis swing of a rolling hand shake; then the awkward and halfhearted embrace and chastely kiss on Kelley's forehead.

His mother advised, "You can give her more of a hug than that, Si. You're not going to see her for a long time."

"Thanks for the obvious, mom," he says with a smirk. When he embraces his mother, it surprises him how small she feels. They hold each other a long time and it embarrasses him that he can feel her breasts through their clothing. He manages to listen to her repeat that she loves him and is proud of him and when she begins to release him he holds on to her. Suddenly he lets her go and she calls after him to tell him to call her when arrives. He smiles and waves and turns and does not look back.

After passing through security, he sits down to put his shoes back on. He sneaks a look back and he can still see them all still there, drifting, unable to see him. He finishes lacing up and makes his way towards the people mover that will take him to his gate. Simon glances back one last time, but no one is there.

I'll be at the gate, was what the text had promised. Simon greatly anticipated seeing his father, but he also felt something else, which he came to admit, was embarrassment. And resentment.

On the one hand, Simon was relieved for his dad that the man had been spared the evident humiliation of coming to a party where the man who had stolen his wife was now living in his own home. At the same time, Simon wonders that his own father has to show his affection in such a dramatic, almost self-centered sort of way. Had Simon still been eleven, it would have seemed genius, two "men" in conspiracy, cloak and dagger, one upping the world. At twenty-two the entire escapade felt pathetic yet grandiose at the same time; his father bought a ticket on the plane for the privilege of having the final audience with his son. And presumptuous, too. Just maybe that's what his father had to do. Poor dad. Acts like he's cool and suave and together, when in fact he's all alone up there. Maybe there's a secret life to dad that I don't know about. Don't want to know about. Mostly though, dad is alone, and he resents not just one but both of his parents for this. Something had happened. Something was neglected between sensible mom and magical dad and he didn't know and did not want to know and the last thing he wanted was to hear from either one of them was their "side", for they seemed eager to be heard, to share at least as much truth as was convenient for them to share, especially without the other one present or invited. Point of fact, neither one had imposed their own story upon him, but Simon imagined he saw it clearly in his mother's big brown guilty eyes, in his father's brave little posturings.

Members of his group were there when he arrived at the gate, shaking his hand. He was distracted, though, on the lookout for his father. Simon told his friends how tired he felt, but it was true, and he put his carry-on bag down and sighed, annoyed that he could not simply relax, but instead had yet one more parent that he felt he had to make feel better about himself. Simon rummages in his bag to find a book, a history of Central America. Before he could sink into its already well grooved pages, Simon looked up and saw a man that clearly was his own father but who seemed to resemble that man but little.

The man he sees is at least five to ten years older than the man Simon spent a weekend with over the winter. The man was almost gaunt with severe lines etching his weathered face. Simon feels shame that his first feeling is one of shame. Who was this man who looked sloppy and ill fitted though he was combed and shaved and tucked? His father's face looked sloppy, heavy laden and dark.

"Dad?" Simon shouts, forgetting himself, rising and embracing the man who holds him tightly and kisses him. Simon kisses him back. "I'm so happy to see you," Simon murmurs, instantly feeling a tug of shame at his emotion.

Ari puts both his hands – which were cold – upon Simon's face, smiles, and winks at him. "If I'm lucky, you might be almost half as glad as I am to see you, son." It was a gesture both rare and revolting.

"It's not a contest, dad," Simon rejoins good naturedly, secretly irritated.

Ari turns, sighs, puts his arm around Simon without facing him. "No, it's not." But then he grins and winks at him. "But you can't even imagine how happy I am, kiddo."

"Yeah, yeah, yeah."

"Yeah, yourself. Let's sit." There were only a few minutes before boarding. Simon decides not to ask any questions, not to ruin the moment, such as it is. They sit in silence a moment, Ari's hand covering his son's. The overhead announcement breaks in, indicating pre-boarding was about to begin for the non-stop flight to Mexico City.

Ari turns to Simon. "I know of course how presumptuous it is of me, but I bought us both tickets together."

"You're getting on the plane?"

"Yes. To Mexico at least."

"You're kidding."

"You really think so?"

"You're going to Mexico?"

"Yeah. Well. At least I'm taking a plane ride."

"Uh. I….well I already have a ticket though."

"With your group, of course. These tickets are different. We're up front with the big shots."

"What are you talking about? We're in the captain's cabin?"

"Hah. Not much room in there. No. Two first class tickets, you and me."

Simon beamed, feeling eleven again, after all. "That's awesome. That must have cost you a fortune."

"Never mind about that. If we can hang out for a bit on the plane and stretch out, that'll be alright."

"I just need to tell our group leader, so they know where I am."

"Of course."

"Well…." Simon wants to ask what (the hell) his father was going to do after they landed in Mexico, but he decides to wait.

As if reading his mind, Ari speaks again. "I really don't know what happens after that. After we land. I haven't had time to really think it through. But I don't think you'll have to worry about your old man getting in your way down there. It's just time to get away for a little bit."

"Time to get away from your great get away," Simon offers.

Ari offers a smile, painful to look at, and claps a hand on Simon's knee. "That's right, son." His father's hands still look

136

vigorous, strong, hirsute with gravitas. "We'll talk a little bit. Why don't you.." he turns to face Simon, "tell me more about what you expect to be doing right after you land."

Simon dutifully starts to talk but he found he wasn't really saying much of anything beyond an ordinal litany of logistical details. And he quietly finds himself wishing that his father would just go away. Was dad really even listening? Why was he really here and what was the matter with him anyway? Why had he not even called or at least texted before not showing up for his going away party, just to tell him he would not be there? Yes, it was painful for everyone. But get over yourself! Simon felt he could smell the past wafting up, the rank of keeping a secret confidence, the subtle plea to take sides despite all surface protestations to the. Even at the age of seven, it had no longer seemed like just a game and he was long past seven already.

His father did not look well. Despite his father's recent reassurance, Simon still fears he will be asked to let his father buddy up join him in his new venture, in which case Simon was prepared to refuse this, hopefully with a smile, but with a resolution to discourage any such insane and unwanted impulses. But there could only be one reason why his father would ever ask such a thing. Because he needed to be rescued. That was what Simon smelled now, the dark side of his father's immaculate self-sufficiency. He sensed it somewhere.

The announcement came, asking for general boarding. "Dad. Let's go. Are you coming?" Ari looks like he isn't, but then he grabs the handle of his small valise on rollers, winks at his son, and they walk together to board.

Theirs were indeed the first two seats on the aircraft, each seat making up its own row at the narrow nose of the plane. Ari looks thoughtful, rubbing his chin. He barely looks up during the flight attendant's demonstration, elegantly demonstrating how to buckle a seat belt with the sinister juxtaposition of the oxygen mask. The attendant was gorgeous, a curvy blonde with feathered hair, like Farrah Fawcett, about his father's age. As the captain announced they were ready for take-off, Ari looks over and throws Simon a wink. He whispers. "When the curtain opens you can see the control panel and the sky."

"Cool."

"You can probably look up the stewardess's skirt, too."

"Nice, dad."

The lady with the feathered hair smiled at both of them while fussing with a small cabinet door, smiling as if she approved of Ari's observation. She looks behind her at the curtain to the cockpit and hearing something that neither father nor son could hear, she disappears behind the curtain.

They lean back anticipating take off. Ari closes his eyes But soon he opens them again and he gives a tired smile just as Simon looks over to check up on him.

"How's it going, dad?" Simon asks nervously.

"Are you excited?"

"Yes, I am."

"This is a moment we'll both remember for a long time, I think."

Simon just nods at him and Ari puts his own hand again over his son's hand. The flight attendant returns and speaks to them.

"Would you like something to drink now?" she offers.

"That's first class. They take your order when you're still on the ground. Tell her what you what, son."

"Do you bring those little bottles of booze?" Simon asks brightly.

"We have a fine selection of premium liquors for you in personally sized bottles."

"All right! I'll have a scotch and rocks with a bottle of red wine with the meal. What the fuck," he says, forgetting himself, turning to his father. To Simon's surprise, Ari orders a ginger ale only. The server winks at them both and moves on to the next row of first class passengers. Father and son make small talk about Simon's itinerary when the captain's voice cracks upon the speakers. "Ladies and gentlemen, this is your captain speaking. We've just been told by ground control that we're going to be delayed for just a bit…..there's…some unanticipated traffic still on the runways, so we're just gonna sit tight and wait our turn. Our flight attendants will soon be coming round with the beverage cart." And the captain briefly details the passengers' snack and drink options. "We apologize for the delay. Just sit back and relax and we'll keep you informed."

Simon offers blandly, "Well. Looks like our flight just got a bit longer."

Ari rubs his face and looks off but then he looks at Simon again and smiles, almost in apology. "Well, kiddo. I was just remembering that time that you and I had finally made that trip together to that world of ours. Our own world. Nog. To the land of Nog."

"What?"

"To the land of Nog."

"The land of..."

"Nog. Remember? Nog." Ari guffaws. "You probably don't. How could you? It was so long ago. When you were, what, five? Six? I used to make up stories before you went to bed."

"I remember."

"And you got to stay up twice as late because first your mother came in and fussed with you. Then I got to come in and hang out. And before I'd kiss you goodnight, you'd be sure that I'd tell you a story or two about the secrets of this world called Nog."

"Nog. I do kind of remember. How'd you come up with that? Was it from eggnog or something silly like that?"

"You came up with it, son. You made it up. You were always making up silly words all the time from the time you could first speak. Maybe all little kids do that, play with the language. Maybe not. But you did."

"Nog."

"Nog. Gog. Bahn. Ging. Gu. Bangawang. You were really, really little then. You just got excited over whatever. A light. A toy. Something colorful. I mean, you were barely a year old when you first started to make up all kinds of words."

"Well yeah, dad. Of course. I was just making baby sounds. I was groping to say something before I could really say it."

"Mmh? No, you were trying to say something. Even then."

139

"I know. That's what I just said."

"I mean you were trying to say something of your own, not just what you thought you heard. You always had a great imagination."

"Dad, I think you just kept remembering those things I said and repeated them back to me."

"Don't contradict your father," Ari says with a sad smirk.

"It must have been Christmas and you gave me some eggnog. You probably spiked it too, so you could laugh while I lolled around all drunk."

"I'm sure I did."

"Yeah, thanks, Dad."

"Oh, you're quite welcome. But. That's not where it came from, the word."

"You're sure."

Ari sighs. "We often had fog over the hills, early mornings. This is in San Jose, of course. I think you were trying to say the word. Fog. Or maybe you didn't hear it right. The other night, I actually dreamed about this place. Nog. Like we finally found a way together there, you and me. To this magical place." Somehow this confession of his father's strikes him as sad.

"Maybe we are, dad. Maybe we're going there now," he offers.

"I doubt it."

"Well I thought you already lived there, in Nog, in your cool house in the woods by the sea."

Ari seems to think about this. "Do you know I can't even hear the ocean from my bedroom? That's the one and only thing I don't like about the place. I'm so close but something always blocks it. It's almost too quiet there." He wants to continue speaking, to tell his son the truth, which is that the dead quiet in his bedroom is intolerable, defeating his splendid solitude and leaving him in a lifeless state without presence, airless and nowhere.

"Dad.....dad, what's happening? You don't look too good, if I can tell you that."

"Just don't talk to your mother like that."

"I wouldn't."

140

"I've been ill the last couple of days. I feel a little better now. Enough at least to get down here thank God."

"Thank Gog!"

"Hah! Yeah."

"I tried calling you and texting you. Several times. Were you that sick?"

"Pretty much, Simon," Ari says turning to him, rubbing his neck. "I'm sorry son. I really am."

"I know you are."

"I got sick on Friday evening…maybe earlier. Not so long after I spoke with you that day." He shakes his head, his jaw clenching. "Well. Late Friday. Then Saturday. I was extremely ill on Saturday. I couldn't sleep. Not until Sunday. And I'm sorry son. I'm so sorry I missed your sendoff party."

"If you were so sick you don't have to be sorry, dad. I didn't know. I just didn't hear from you." Simon guesses in his heart that his father is lying to him but in a way that is perversely truthful, enough at least to be a preferable version of the truth than a factual accounting of dismal and unseemly facts that he had no desire to hear. He worried about his father sometimes and therefore he is all the more glad he is going away, to be rid of feeling responsible for him. Then again, here is father still sits, as if he really were about to attach himself to Simon on his new venture. It occurred to Simon that however glad he had been to see his father, it had mainly been with the purpose of saying Goodbye.

The attendant comes to them, well-rehearsed, asking to describe to them the specials for the evening.

"First class, son. Want some airplane steak?"

"Heck yeah."

"Oh, you won't be disappointed," chimes the attendant. As she explain their superior selection of prime cuts, the sauces and greens, Simon observes that his father already looks disappointed. Ari smiles wanly at the woman, barely noticing her it seems. "It seems we're gonna be delayed for a little while longer. But we'll bring you your drinks right away."

"Thank you," Ari replies.

The drinks soon arrive. Ari stirs and stares. "Dad."

"Yeah, kiddo."

"How'd you get so sick?"

"How? How does anybody get sick?"

Simon shrugs. "I don't know. Have you been hanging out in the rain?" he asks archly.

Ari looks a little lost and leans over his hands. "I had an accident over the weekend. I fell ill, I think, after that?"

"An accident?" Simon lowers his voice. "Was anyone else hurt?"

"It wasn't a car accident, if that's what you mean?"

"Well, what happened?"

Ari seems to consider this. He closes his eyes and shakes his head rubbing his closed lids. "Well. I fell while jogging. On the back trail into Trinidad. I wasn't really hurt. But you were, because I missed your party."

"Dad. Enough already with the apologies. I get it. You're really sorry."

"I am."

"Maybe it was all for the best. "

Ari looks at him, sensing the irritation in his son. "Really? I don't know. Maybe."

"What are you gonna do after we land in Mexico City? Are you coming with me to Honduras?"

Ari remains silent for a moment, pinching his lip between his thumb and forefinger. "No. Of course not." This time Simon believes him. Great relief. Salted with guilt and melancholy. "No. I'll be going right back on the next plane going home."

"Yeah? Well, dad. That's a very expensive way you chose to say goodbye."

"I was never going to crash your party in Honduras. But I was thinking I might travel in Mexico or Panama or Costa Rica, maybe. Costa Rica, I hear is pretty easy for Americans to survive in. It's tempting. Very tempting. Costa Rica sounds like just the kind of place an idle American can do some thinking. But….somehow I really can't. I have some things to do."

"Like what, dad?"

"Hey, you remember my friend Albert? I've known him since college. Nice man. Maybe you don't remember."

"Was he that tall skinny dude that used to go hiking with us? The one who used to swear a lot?"

"That's right. That's him. We used to take you with us into the mountains. We took you overnight camping too, even backpacking once. Do you remember? We camped under the stars. In the Sierras."

"It was cold. I remember that. I remember Albert telling ghost stories by this fire he made. 'Where's my golden arm?'" Simon recalls, his voice turning icy in channeling the fond memory of a young boy's over stimulated imagination on a dark starry night, "That creeped me out." But he also remembers feeling initiated into the company of men, protected by his father and his father's most trusted lieutenant.

"Hah. Oh yeah. Where the hell's my golden arm? You made him repeat that. Then you couldn't sleep."

"Hell, he grabs me at the end and screams, 'You've got it!'"

"Maybe that was a little much."

"Actually, it was pretty awesome. What made you think of him?"

"He says 'Hello'. That's all. He lives in Redding now."

"Oh. You just talked with him?"

"I made it out to his place on Sunday night and we visited until this afternoon, although I slept the first day or so. I guess I didn't want to make the whole drive all at once. It was good to see him. Anyway, he says, 'Hello'. Remembers you pretty well."

"That must have been nice. Honestly, I only remember him a little bit. Mostly the golden arm stuff."

"Of course. He remembers you. We were talking about that backpacking trip. We remember how quiet you got while you were out with us. You know you were always one who could talk up a blue streak about anything that was on your mind, what you thought of this or that, who said what at school. But not when you got out in the woods with us.

143

We didn't have to remind you to look at where you were. No talking. No game boy. No headsets. It was me and Albert who made all the noise. And then we all got quiet, especially when it got a little steep. There was just a little wind, much of the time. Maybe. The crunch of a twig. The sound of our own breath. Albert took the lead. I walked behind you. We were protecting you, of course. But after a while it was like….it was almost like you were protecting us. I liked to watch you watch over everything and to watch you listening to the silence. And so we got real quiet, too. We had to."

"Dad."

"Mmm."

"I don't know really know what you're talking about." But I'm feeling really uncomfortable with what you're saying.

"Yeah, I guess I don't really know either."

"So how is Albert, anyway?" Simon asks just to be polite.

"Thoughtful of you to ask. He's not really doing so great. I meant to tell you. At least not his health. He has stage four lung cancer."

"Oh…that's terrible."

"He quit smoking, too, over twenty years ago. But it still caught up with him. Now he's even skinnier. He's had chemo, lost weight and he's slow moving. But he's at home now, and he intends to stay there." Ari turns inward, picturing his old friend, tall, emaciated, baggy jeans, a red and black plaid shirt hanging loose upon a ratty, torn t-shirt, and a John Deere cap covering his head, matted coils of thin hair pasted on his scalp, standing on his own porch, having just tried to do ten minutes worth of gardening, a staring, cavernous smile, three days of white stubble, a front tooth missing from a row of yellow and black razorous nubs. "He's taking a break from all treatment. Except Vicadin."

"Taking a break?"

"He'll most likely die very soon, Simon."

"Hell."

"You know what. He's OK with it."

"Yeah? That's good." Simon slowly says. He can't think of anything else to say.

144

"I feel like a moron, Simon. I went to his place asking for *his* help, asking him to take care of me."

"He's your friend," Simon shrugs.

"I remember one time, he and I were out hiking, just the two of us, and we went well above the snow line, and neither one of us were really prepared. Down below it was eighty degrees, but there was a lot of snow and ice up where we were. And I slipped and...." Ari thinks about that moment. He remembers clearly his own detached acceptance that he might die right then and there. But he wanted to see his son again and that was enough. Ari decides that, of course, he is not about to share as much with Simon. "Albert really saved my butt that day." Ari stares at the blank air cabin walls. "Yeah. So I decided that I'm going back to Redding instead and help my friend until he passes. If he'll let me."

Albert had listened to the truth and the whole truth, not only about the dead woman, but about his wounded lover, his useless rage at Sabrina, his displaced resentment towards his harmless boss, as well as other useless and inexplicable emotions, ideas, fears, and obsessions. And his friend, his dying friend, just sat there and took it. Just took it until Ari finally took to his bed in the cold and empty spare room, peaceful and ready, passed out for the rest of the night and all through the next day as well. He had the vague memory of the heater going on and of Albert shuffling quietly to place an extra blanket on him in the middle of the night.

No, he would certainly not continue on to far off uncharted and magical little broken countries. He would return and if allowed, stay on with Albert until it was time to bury what was left of him, because there was no one else to do it, and because he wanted to, whether it was weeks or months, whatever it was. He had all summer. Actually, he had a good deal longer than that, for he would not likely be returning to the college.

He'd sell the house and maybe he'd gladly consign himself to living in Albert's modest home outside of Redding and he'd stay real quiet and there would be no more fog. Maybe someone would still hire him to be an on-line business instructor. If he were lucky, he would get to sit in the sunshine instead of the rain, exposed to the cleansing plainness of the day. But he'd talk to his dead friend and they'd drink beer together at every sunset, and Ari would drink the bottle for his friend as well and sit out on the porch until late at night and he'd have no memory of anything except for his friend and for the day that his son would come back to him. "Later I'll go back to Trinidad where I've got some business to take care of."

Simon looks at his father. There were so many questions that Simon wanted to ask but for which he did not really want to hear the answers. The flight attendant returns to them with an anxious look on her face. She prepares a smile for Ari and putting her hand on his arm, she gently tells him. "Are you Mr. Fisher?"

"Yes, I am."

"The captain wanted to speak to you for a moment. It will only take a moment," she says, glancing at Simon.

"Of course," Ari says with no hint of surprise.

"You're a celebrity, dad."

Ari winks at his son. "Don't down that drink all at once."

No one suggests to Simon that he join his father in the captain's cabin. The eleven year old in him still believes his father must be a celebrity to be summoned to a private audience with the pilot, but the twenty-two year old man suspects that something is wrong.

Indeed, before he can settle into daydreaming or worry, his father reappears wearing a smile way too big for him. The flight attendant watches him. Ari reaches into the overhead compartment to take down his shoulder bag. Then he sits back down without putting on his seatbelt. "I have to go, Ari. I'm sorry."

"What? What are you talking about?"

"It's OK, son. I knew that this could happen. I wanted to see you and say goodbye and I did. So everything's OK. And you'll be back, bigger and stronger, and we'll be two men together then."

"Why on earth do you have to go? What happened?"

"It's Albert. He's back in the hospital and he has no family, so I need to be there. I'd rather stay with you but you're gonna be just fine. But Albert needs me now."

146

"Oh."

"It's a strange way to say goodbye, I know. Look, I only have half a minute," and Ari looks over at the flight attendant and holds up a single finger as if to assure her that he is indeed about to leave. "I was going to raise a toast, but this will have to do." He takes a breath and tells his son. "I love you my boy. I know I don't tell you often enough. Or hardly ever. But you're a good kid. You know what? Correct that. You're my kid, but I know you're a man Simon. You're a man. You're a very, very good man. And I am so very, very proud of you."

After father and son embrace and Ari takes leave of his
bewildered son, the flight attendant escorts him down the narrow inner
ramp that leads to the gate. He turns to her. "I apologize to you and to
everyone for the inconvenience."

She looks at him as if about to say something but she doesn't say
anything. As he leaves the plane, a member of the airline is right there
and wordlessly and needlessly walks with him the few feet to where
three plain clothes detectives, two men and a woman, are waiting for
him. One of them he recognizes as Bud Cameron's son. Before any of
them can speak, Ari greets them. "This is better than I deserve. Thank
you for allowing me to say goodbye to my son."

"That's quite a goodbye, Mr. Fisher," the male detective offers
without introducing himself. "Most people spare themselves the expense
by doing so at the gate."

"Of course. Look, I don't expect you to believe me when I tell
you that I was going to come right back and once my son and I landed in
Mexico. But you're here now and I'm ready to answer all of your
questions."

"Yes," the woman says. "Well we do have a few for you. And
we can actually get started just at the other end of the hallway."

"Good. Officer Cameron! I did not expect to see you here."

"He's not exactly here officially, but you should be glad that he
is." And they walk together briskly like peers on a mission. The airline
representative follows them as well and it is this man alone whose
presence Ari slightly resents.

Ari remains silent which is easy to do since no one is speaking to
him. They cross the length of one causeway and turn at a small plain
elevator that is barely noticeable, used no doubt only by the staff. The
airline man takes out a key and turns something on the elevator key pad.
The cab rises to the next level, one never used by the public. They walk
halfway down a smaller, empty hallway, until the representative turns to
a door on the right, unlocks an office and the four of them walk through a

148

little waiting area and into a plain inner conference room. The airline man turns on the light, moves a couple of chairs closer to the table, and asks if they need anything. The woman asks for water and the man affirms that he will bring water for everyone. They sit down.

The man who is unknown to Ari, introduces himself. "I'm Detective Janis of the SJPD. This is Detective Ramsey. You already know Officer Cameron from CHP in Humboldt county."

"Yes, of course. We met a few nights ago and he was exceptionally courteous."

"You seem to know why we are here, Mr. Fisher."

"I would be grateful if you would briefly tell me."

"Mr. Fisher, we have identified you as a person of interest in the apparent disappearance of Mrs. Victoria Ng -"

"Yes, of course. That's exactly what I thought. Mrs. Ng, unfortunately is deceased. She died, so far as I can tell, from a massive heart attack. I'm not a doctor, of course, but she told me as much at dinner that night that she had already suffered several such attacks before and that she was at high risk for sudden death at almost any moment."

"Are you saying she was with you when she died?"

"Certainly. We were having sex at the moment she passed – intercourse to be precise. And this was the thing, more than any other that I was ashamed of, and wanted to cover up. In my stupid panic, I buried her and I'll try my best to show you where the body is. For whatever its worth, I tell you that I did not kill this woman or otherwise cause her any intentional harm, and the sex itself was certainly consensual." On this last point – indeed, on any of the points he had tried to make; no intent to kill, no intent to harm, no intent to sexually assault - Ari could never be absolutely certain. It occurred to him that he had always been completely uncertain as to what had actually happened during those moments, however few or many they were, when his Id had been unleashed in a black out, now forever buried from his conscious memory.

Ari looks at the faces of his interrogators. They seem surprised by his confession. Cameron clearly believes him, Ramsey less so, and Janis is impossible to read. "Look, I know we're just getting started.

149

But I'll tell you anything you want and I'll tell you the truth. I'm done with covering anything up anymore. I'm just grateful that I finally got some sleep and grateful that I got to say goodbye to my son."

The inquiry continues but after less than an hour, Janis turns to Cameron. "What do you think? It's your neighborhood, not ours."

"We'll have to get Del Norte involved. I think he's fine with me, though."

Cameron is mild enough to him and even lets Ari ride in the front seat of his CHP car as they rapidly head north on the I5. The day is warm and sunny. "We're gonna take you up on your offer to show us where you left the body. We already have a pretty good idea. Some hikers found some personal items thought to be hers."

"From her luggage. Yes."

"Tell me something, the truth…"

"Yes…she was there."

"She was where?"

"In the trunk. When you pulled me over. Her body was in the trunk. I'm sorry." Ari looks over and he can see that Cameron looks flushed and angry, as if what happened that night was a personal insult to him. "You were very gracious to me and you were looking out for my safety and for the safety of - "

"Shut up," Cameron quietly commands. "Damn it," the cop mutters to himself. Ari understands that he has personally let down this young man. Not just his father. "After I let you go that night. You kept going northbound. After I told you like fifty times to go home."

"Yes. The body was already in my trunk. I no longer had any choice about it."

"I should have guessed you were hiding something."

"How could you guess such a thing?"

"I just should have. I don't suppose you've made any donations to the Salvation Army after all."

"No."

"Son of a bitch." Cameron isn't calling Ari names. He's merely speaking words of weariness, of feigned incredulity.

"I went up north," Ari explains. "After I finished up there, I stopped in Crescent City. Somehow after that I made it back down." Ari leaves out his black out that miraculously delivered him to Redwood state park. "I haven't even been back home since then. I just couldn't go back. I've been in Redding with a sick friend since Saturday."

For a long time Cameron says nothing. "Since you seem to like it so much in Crescent City, you might just love it in Pelican Bay. I hear on a clear day you can even see the ocean." Ari gets quiet. And numb. "You can post bail, I suppose."

"Am I under arrest?"

Cameron sighs. "No." But it's a 'No' lacking in finality, a 'No' suspended in the mist. "Not yet. I don't decide what the charge will be. But it has to be something, Mr. Fisher. You can't just decide to go dump a body wherever you want to and pretend it never existed. Even if you just saw it lying there on the ground, and that's not what happened at all. And you don't go to that extent to cover up whatever you covered up if it wasn't something awful, now do you. It's not right. You don't walk away from this, Mr. Fisher. That's for damn sure." "

Ari says nothing at first. "I know you're right. Why did you come up? They would have had to bring me back, I suppose."

Cameron signals with his left hand to veer into another lane. "Not necessarily. I was the one who stopped you that night. And I figured I could help keep this thing quiet until we at least figured out what the hell was going on."

"OK. Well, I think I'm kinda glad you did."

"I didn't do it for you."

"Of course."

"You should have gone straight home that night, Mr. Fisher."

"I told you. I was already too far gone by then."

Again the silence. Then he turns to Ari again. Not unkindly he asks of him, "When was it not too late for you? When was it not too late for any of us?" He was referring no doubt to how Ari Fisher had compromised the college and his father.

"I think it was when I fell down."

"When you fell?"

151

"I was jogging that morning. I had had almost no sleep the night before. Already I was behaving badly, staying out late the night before, driving up and down the coast for no reason - sober, mind you - losing sleep. I decided to go for a run that morning and I fell. I was lucky I wasn't seriously hurt. At that exact moment - certainly before perhaps, but for some reason I keep coming back to that moment in particular - that was the moment I had already decided that as soon as I could hobble back, that I would forsake all other obsessions, that I would turn off all the phones, all my devices, turn off everything, turn off my mind, and that I would crawl into my bed, and that I would hide, blameless under the covers for the rest of the day. Well. Until it was time. If I had done that at least, I think the world would have looked different to me, different enough that the rest of that day and night would have turned out differently as well."

"Are you sure about that?"

Ari thinks about this. "No. But I would have gotten some sleep at least."

"And why didn't you?"

"Go to bed you mean? You realize it's pointless to ask. This is how it turned out."

"I know. It's true." They pass a sign that reads, Redding - 28 miles. "But why?"

"I don't know. Because I didn't want to. Because I couldn't let myself just be. Something like that."

"I don't think you're a murderer, Mr. Fisher. I can't rule that possibility out either. I really don't know what you are. But I do know that you let down a whole lot of people. Including her."

"I know."

After a few minutes of silence, Officer Cameron speaks again, a slow building random soliloquy, as if speaking to himself, talking of all things about his father, memories both fond and remote. He talks as if he needs to talk, either to escape the moment or because he must unburden himself to someone in whose presence he can no longer feel any embarrassment. Ari lets his eyes close but immediately opens them

152

again, willing himself to bear witness to whatever testimony will issue from his keeper.

"I appreciate you talking to me," is all Ari can say. Cameron looks at him as if surprised that another sentient being is in the car with him after all, or instead as if in disaccord with the idea that his words were ever meant for Ari to hear them. A few minutes later, Ari clears his throat and speaks again. "We're coming up on Redding. I have a childhood friend here who's dying. I wonder if I'll get to see him again or take care of him." He realizes he says this as if Cameron would decide to leave him at Albert's doorstep, adjudicated to live out his sentence in love and service to the dying.

"Well, if so," Cameron says, "your friend might be one more person you've disappointed."

".....Yes. You're right."

They arrive at the junction of the 5 and the 299 and they turn left, heading west, escaping the monotony of the flat lands. They witness the sun setting behind the hills, gentle and carpeted green with trees. The dimming sky still holds its brilliance, cream and golden hued. "Mr. Fisher, I believe you're gonna be our guest at the station tonight. Maybe just for tonight. It's not Pelican Bay. And you're welcome to contact your attorney."

"I suppose that depends on whether I'm under arrest."

"We'll see. You seem to be a flight risk. Wouldn't you say?"

"Not anymore."

They approach the hills and the turning of the road and Ari realizes that although it has only been three days, he already feels as if it has been weeks or months since he has last seen his beloved Redwoods. These are still home for him. The school is gone to him, that seems certain. His house is haunted. Tainted. But the trees and the land, they are still his home, whether he gets to live amongst them or not; the trees and the land and the living mist that animates them both. The fog.

Cameron turns on the radio.

153

Edan Benn Epstein lives in Southern California with his wife and two cats. He can be contacted at ebepstein@sbcglobal.net. His novels include Empty Sky (1997), Subterranean Green (2011), Fog (2012), The Anteater (2014) and Afternoon of the Faun (2015), all of which will be available through Amazon before the end 2016. His sixth novel, The Rite of Spring, the epic yet intimate story of four dysfunctional siblings and four generations careening through life from the present day until the unrecognizable world of 2080, will be available in 2017. **For further updates, like us on Facebook at Edan Benn Epstein.**

AVAILABLE NOW ON AMAZON! **THE ANTEATER - an existential thriller. "A spiritually redemptive act."**

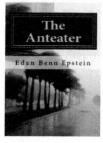

The Anteater, Epstein's fourth novel, follows the hopes, fears, and secrets of seven men working for a third rate messenger service in Los Angeles in 1985. Over the course of three days in November, a perfect storm — both literal and emotional — changes their lives forever. Magic intertwines with grim reality in a tale of deep inner longing forever just one step ahead of existential checkmate. The novel integrates seven stories, all of them haunted by the city scape dregs of 1980s Los Angeles. *"Delves into areas of the human psyche that fiction rarely explores." "A spiritually redemptive act"* **$12.95 in paperback on Amazon.com. (296 pages) Only $2.99 on Kindle.**

AVAILABLE NOW ON AMAZON! THE WAY TO NOD - Short stories and novelettes from the edge!

A young man fights the insane urge to throw champagne into the face of his beloved's father; a woman at work copes in paranoid ways; an underling's misplaced resentment towards his boss pushes him into a deadly street confrontation. The title story follows a desperate escape from a nightmare dystopia in quest of a peaceful land that no one knows for sure really exists. Enjoy these and other tales from the edge. **Only $6.95 in paperback.** *Only 99 cents on Kindle!*

AVAILABLE NOW ON AMAZON! **FOG** - *An idyllic tale of mayhem set in the California Redwoods.*

Only $8.95 in paperback on Amazon. (154 pages) *Only 99 cents on Kindle!*

Made in the USA
Middletown, DE
06 July 2022

68585140R00089